Silent Witness

The camera stayed on Jon's face.

It looked as if he was in a hallway or something. There was a door behind him, and no one else seemed to be around.

The camera zoomed up close on Jon's face, and Lucy would have enjoyed it, except for his expression: Jon was furious.

His mouth moved, and he was talking, saying something in anger. His gray eyes were dark, Lucy noticed, the way they'd been the night before.

The camera kept rolling, recording it all.

Then Jon moved, walking quickly toward the camera with his hand out. His hand filled the lens until all Lucy could see was darkness.

Point Horror

SILENT WITNESS

Carol Ellis

SCHOLASTIC

Scholastic Children's Books,
Scholastic Publications Ltd,
7-9 Pratt Street, London NW1 OAE, UK

Scholastic Inc.,
555 Broadway, New York, NY 10012-3999, USA

Scholastic Canada Ltd,
123 Newkirk Road, Richmond Hill,
Ontario, Canada L4C 3G5

Ashton Scholastic Pty Ltd,
PO Box 579, Gosford, New South Wales,
Australia

Ashton Scholastic Ltd,
Private Bag 92801, Penrose, Auckland,
New Zealand

First published in the US by Scholastic Inc., 1994
First published in the UK by Scholastic Publications Ltd, 1994

Copyright © Carol Ellis, 1994

ISBN: 0 590 55716 5

Printed by Cox & Wyman Ltd, Reading, Berks

10 9 8 7 6 5 4 3 2 1

SILENT WITNESS

Chapter 1

Lucy Monroe woke suddenly, breaking through layers of sleep with a smile on her face. She'd heard the rhythmic thump of the basketball again. Her next-door neighbor, Allen Torrance, was in his driveway, shooting baskets. When she was trying to study and not getting anywhere, the monotonous sound could drive Lucy crazy. This time, it made her smile.

But this time, the sound wasn't real. Five-foot, seven-inch Allen wasn't in his driveway, imagining himself twelve inches taller. Allen was six feet under the ground, buried three weeks ago. Dead for a month.

She'd dreamed it again, Lucy thought, sitting up and blinking in the darkness. Of all the things she remembered about Allen, the sound of his basketball stuck with her the most, even when she was asleep.

They'd been neighbors since second grade. Only ten years, but it seemed like forever. They'd never been anything more than friends, but they'd been good friends. Lucy had never thought about it much until he died. Allen was just there — teasing her, always teasing her. But sometimes cheering her up, like after her first disastrous driving lesson.

Then suddenly, he wasn't there.

Was it worse because his death had been such a surprise? He'd gone walking alone, up on a high, crumbling, cement embankment. Dumb, but only because of what happened. Everybody walked there. But only Allen fell. Now nobody walked there.

If he'd had some long, horrible illness, instead of that quick fall, would it have made it easier to get used to?

Maybe, but she'd still miss him. Even his teasing.

Enough of this.

Lucy peered at the clock on her bedside table. Four in the morning, and pitch-dark. Two and a half hours until she had to get up and get ready for school. Moe, her gray and white cat, lifted his head from his sleeping spot on the end of the bed and stared at her: Was she going to disturb him some more or was she going to settle down? Lucy flipped the pillow over and stretched out again, but she couldn't go back to sleep.

It wasn't a remembered sound that kept her awake, but a presence. Not imagined or dreamed of, but a real one. A presence in her room, over in the corner. It had been there for two weeks, gathering dust.

Face it, Lucy told herself. Once you look at it and do something about it, maybe the dreams will go away.

It was late fall, almost Halloween, and the bedroom was cold. Lucy threw back the covers and pulled on her quilted robe, so well-padded it was like being wrapped in a thick blue cocoon. (Allen had seen her in it one morning when she went out to get the paper and called her the Pillsbury Doughgirl.)

Tugging on a pair of heavy socks, Lucy stood up and pulled her long brown hair free from the neck of the robe. She was right in front of the window, the one that looked across the side yard to the Torrances' house.

She hadn't pulled her shade and, through the gauzy white curtain, she thought she saw a thin pinpoint of light. It was coming from a chink in the blinds on the Torrances' family room window.

Was it really there? Allen's parents were gone. Trying to ease their pain by traveling.

Stepping close to her window, Lucy pulled the curtain aside and stared across the yard. She held her breath, as if that would make the light shine again.

She let out her breath and looked until her breath fogged the window. Then she wiped away the mist and looked some more. She saw nothing but the shadowy hulk of the Torrance house. Dark, with no light shining behind the blinds.

A ghost, Lucy thought. Just like the thud of the basketball. There's only one way to get rid of it.

Dropping the curtain, Lucy skirted her bed and went to the closet. She opened the door and pulled the light string. A weak light spilled out across the floor, stretching to the corner of the room where a large cardboard box had sat for two weeks.

Kneeling down in front of the box, Lucy remembered:

It was a week after Allen's funeral. The doorbell rang and Lucy answered it. Mrs. Tor-

rance was standing on the porch, holding the box.

Lucy hadn't seen her since the funeral. She was short, with bright, snapping dark eyes that Allen had inherited. Her eyes weren't bright that day.

"We're going away for a while," Mrs. Torrance said after Lucy invited her in. She put down the box in the hall and straightened up. "I have a favor to ask, Lucy."

Lucy nodded, hoping she looked helpful. She wanted to be, but she kept eyeing the box and not liking what she saw.

"Tell me if it's too much to ask," Mrs. Torrance said. "I was going through Allen's things. I kept some, of course. Some I want to give away, to his friends, but I couldn't bear calling each one and asking. So I thought you could take what you want — if you want anything, and please don't feel like you have to — and then give the rest away for me."

And Lucy said, "Of course I'll do it for you. I'll be glad to do it."

A lie. It wasn't too much to ask, but she wasn't really glad to do it. She didn't even want to look at the stuff, so she set it in a corner of her room and covered it with an old sheet.

Coward, Lucy thought now. If Allen's mom could make herself pack it up, you can make yourself look at it and give it away.

A soft thud came from the bedside. Purring, Moe joined Lucy and rubbed against her leg. She scratched between his ears for a moment, then pulled the sheet off the box and started taking things out.

Three posters: One Michael Jordan, two old movie posters. Allen had planned to become a filmmaker one day.

Fifteen comic books: Collector's items? Lucy had no idea.

One videotape: Allen's video camera was always glued to his eye.

Some photographs: From Allen's pre-video days, when he was hooked on photography. One of her, getting ready to throw a snowball at him.

Twenty CDs: Lucy grinned, remembering how she'd shut her window whenever Allen blasted his stereo.

Hundreds of baseball cards: Allen had collected them like crazy until he was about fourteen. Sometimes Lucy would give him the money for them and he'd give her the bubble gum.

And the basketball.

Lucy rocked back on her heels, already thinking about who might like what. She picked up the videotape. No title. The plastic casing had a scratch on it shaped like the letter Z.

Groggy but curious, she left her room and went down the hall, past her parents' room and into the den. The cat padded silently along beside her. Switching on a lamp, Lucy turned on the television and the VCR, and settled into the recliner to watch Allen's "movie."

First up was last spring's junior class car wash. Lots of kids getting as wet and soapy as the cars. There was Jenny Berger, Lucy's best friend, aiming the hose at Lucy. The camera panned to a shot of Robert Owen, directing traffic. Robert had organized the car wash. He was in on everything; he'd need a whole yearbook to himself just to list his activities.

There was no sound, and Lucy remembered Allen saying something about adding his own commentary one day.

A few more minutes of the car wash, and then the setting changed. People walking down a street. Some of them looked embarrassed by the camera, some of them mugged for it.

Another scene change. Allen's patio; his big Fourth of July party. A shaky shot of Suzanne Gold and Brad Forest slow-dancing, their arms wrapped around each other. Tiny Suzanne and huge Brad, the great love match. They'd been going together for years. Lucy liked them, but she didn't really know them, not as individuals. It was always Brad and Suzanne, never one or the other.

More street scenes. Then a lot of wobbly shots of treetops and sky. Allen must have been lying on his back.

Lucy yawned. It was just past five. Almost an hour and a half of sleep left if she could conk out real fast before it got light. Yawning again, she switched off the VCR and the television and headed down the hall to her room. The cat was already back on the bed, curled into a ball.

Outside, the thick darkness was just beginning to change. Soon it would be dark gray, then lighter, then the bright white of morning. Lucy snapped down the shades, took off her robe and got into bed, turning her back on the bedside window.

*　*　*

Across the side yard, behind the blinds of the Torrance house, the thin beam of light moved from room to room, a small, searching beacon in the darkness. If Lucy had looked, she would have seen it.

But Lucy was fast asleep.

Chapter 2

At Bridgetown High later that morning, Lucy shifted a big paper shopping bag from one hand to the other and brushed some raindrops off her hair. The darkness of the night before had turned into light gray, no brighter, and now it was sprinkling outside.

"You couldn't have been shopping already," Jenny Berger said, looking at the bag. "It's only eight-thirty."

"I haven't been anywhere," Lucy said as they started toward their lockers. "This is some of the stuff Allen's mom gave me. Remember, I told you about it?"

Jenny nodded. Her hair, almost the same length and shade of brown as Lucy's, swung forward onto her shoulders. "You finally looked at it, huh?" she asked.

"It wasn't as bad as I thought it would be," Lucy said. "Maybe because I did it at four this morning and I was too groggy to get all upset. Anyway, now that I went through it, I'm ready to give most of it away."

"What kind of stuff is it?"

"Comic books, and some posters," Lucy said. "CDs. A videotape — it's not like what you do," she added. Jenny was in the video club and determined to work in television or film someday. "I only watched a little of it, but it's kind of fun — the car wash, the July Fourth party, a bunch of people walking on the sidewalk, stuff like that."

Jenny smiled. "Allen drove everybody crazy with that camera."

"It doesn't have any sound, though," Lucy said. "We don't get to hear what anyone's saying. Anyway," she went on, "I'm keeping that, and a couple of CDs. But I brought the rest of the stuff with me." They were at her locker now, and she set down the shopping bag. "Why don't you see if there's anything you want?"

While Lucy hung up her jacket and fished through the locker for a notebook, Jenny knelt down and looked in the bag. "This feels very strange," she said. "Going through Allen's stuff, I mean."

"Why do you think I kept putting it off?"

Lucy asked. She finally found the notebook and pulled it out, accidentally knocking her old school-bus-yellow rain poncho off its hook. She'd bought a new poncho — green, and not stiff like the old one, which had been hanging in her locker since a rainy day back in September.

"Hey, can I borrow that?" Jenny asked, standing up. "I promised my mother I'd drop the car off at the garage at lunch. I'll have to walk back to school and it's going to pour."

Thunder rumbled outside, as if in agreement.

"You can have it," Lucy said, picking up the poncho and handing it to Jenny. "I feel like a neon sign in that thing. What'd you take?" she asked, looking at the CDs Jenny was holding.

"Just these two." Jenny held up the CDs for Lucy to see. "Actually, I already have them. I guess I just want something to remember him by."

"I know," Lucy said. She felt tears starting in her eyes, and blinked them back. "You want a poster? The baseball cards, maybe?"

Jenny laughed a little, blinking back her own tears. "If nobody here wants the cards, take them to a thrift shop or someplace like that.

I'd better hurry," she added as the warning bell rang. "Listen, when you're done with the video, I'd like to see it."

"I guess everybody would," Lucy said.

"So give it to me and I'll edit it." Jenny was halfway down the hall, walking backward. "I could put a music track on it, too. We can get everybody together and have a showing."

Like a wake, Lucy thought, as Jenny disappeared around the corner.

Walking into the cafeteria at lunchtime, Lucy remembered what it had been like the day after Allen died. Kids who didn't know him thought it was sad, but kind of exciting, too. They ate fast and talked with their mouths full, asking each other questions about what had happened.

Kids who knew him, especially the ones who knew him well, either picked at their food or didn't touch it at all. They talked in quick bursts. Then they'd get quiet, staring at each other or at the tabletop.

Brad had looked confused and glum that day, and Lucy remembered being annoyed. It was the same pained expression he got when a teacher gave a pop quiz. Then she felt ashamed of herself for thinking that. She wasn't crazy about Brad, but he had been Allen's friend. He was hurting.

Suzanne had looked furious. Her small face was pinched and she'd shrugged off Brad's arm, which was usually draped across her shoulder. Lucy had finally decided she was trying not to cry.

Jenny didn't bother to try: She'd cried plenty, like Lucy.

Robert's eyes were red, as if he'd been studying most of the night. Since he was an ace student, he probably had been. But Lucy thought maybe he'd cried a little, too.

Lucy didn't know if Jon had cried. He hadn't been in the cafeteria that day.

Jonathan Eden. Lucy loved the sound of his name. Just hearing it, and thinking about him, gave her a thrill.

He'd moved to Bridgetown in August. Lucy didn't know how many friends he'd made, but one of them was Allen. Late in August, and from then on until Allen died, Jon would come over to the Torrance house and he and Allen would shoot baskets together. If Lucy was in her bedroom, she'd hear them. Sometimes they'd joke around, shouting out insults about the quality of each other's playing. Most of the time all she heard was the basketball.

Sometimes she'd look out the window and watch them play. Jon was taller than Allen, but not as fast. His hair was dark blond and his eyes were blue. Or gray. Lucy couldn't really remember. She hadn't seen him up close more than a couple of times. He'd been friends with Allen, but that was about all she knew about him. He seemed kind of distant. Not un-friendly, really. Just kind of cool and . . . mysterious. Lucy wished she could get to know him.

Jon wasn't in any of Lucy's classes and, whenever she saw him in the halls, he was usually alone. It was probably awful, moving to a new school in your senior year. She won-dered if Allen had been his only good friend so far.

Scanning the crowded cafeteria, Lucy spot-ted Suzanne and Brad. And Robert. But not Jon. He wasn't here today, either. She knew this was his lunch period. Maybe he'd gone out. Seniors could do that, but most of them didn't bother since there wasn't much time.

Lucy had brought her lunch. It was in the shopping bag with Allen's things. She bought a carton of juice and threaded her way through the noisy crowd to the table where Robert was sitting.

"What'd you bring, a whole roast beef?" Robert asked, looking at the big bag. He had a bunch of notes spread out around him. AP History, the only class they shared.

Lucy pulled out a chair and slid one of Robert's notebooks aside. She set the shopping bag on the floor beside her and took out her food — a sandwich and an apple. "This is my lunch," she said. "The stuff in the bag is Allen's."

Robert's hand had been reaching for her apple. Now he pulled it back and frowned at her. "What do you mean?"

"Allen's mom gave me some of his things to give away to friends," Lucy explained. "So I brought some of it with me."

Robert's glance strayed to the shopping bag.

"You two were pretty good friends," Lucy said, giving him the apple. "I thought you might want something."

Robert turned the apple over in his hands, still frowning.

"Look, you don't have to take anything," Lucy said. "The stuff isn't special. Well, except that it was Allen's."

Robert shook his head. "Sorry, I didn't mean to make you think I don't want something. I guess I just didn't expect this. Now, I mean."

"I know, it's my fault," Lucy said. "I let the stuff sit in my room for a long time."

Robert nodded, his brown eyes full of understanding. He ate some of the apple. "Okay," he said, swallowing. "What treasures did Allen leave?"

Lucy smiled. "Baseball cards, about a thousand of them. Posters. Comic books, CDs." She didn't mention the basketball. "A video, but I'm keeping that. Remember how he was always using the camera? He got us all on tape. Jenny thinks I should have a showing."

Robert laughed. "What's it rated?"

"PG, so far. But . . ." Lucy tilted her head toward the table where Brad and Suzanne were sitting. "There's a shot of them dancing at the Fourth party," she said with a grin. "No daylight between them."

"Sounds like R to me," Robert said.

"So what would you like?" Lucy asked, pulling the shopping bag into her lap. "The baseball cards, maybe? Allen collected them — maybe some of them are valuable by now."

"Maybe, but I wouldn't sell them." Robert

leaned over the table and peered into the bag. "Hey, his basketball," he said. "Who's that for?"

"You, if you want it," Lucy said. "It's not like there's a will or anything. I'm just letting people pick." She hoped Robert wouldn't pick the basketball.

"Michael Jordan," Robert said, unrolling a poster. "Allen's favorite guy. Maybe I'll take this. I'm a better fan than a player." He rolled the poster back up. "Thanks, Lucy."

"Okay." Lucy finished her sandwich and stood up. "I'm going to see if Suzanne and Brad want something."

Robert was already looking at his history notes again.

"Hey, Robert?" Lucy said. "Before our next test, could I borrow your notes?"

"Not a chance." Robert didn't glance up. "But I'll make copies of them for you," he added, and Lucy heard the smile in his voice.

She laughed. "Thanks. See you, Robert." He wasn't usually so generous with his notes. In fact, he could act kind of superior sometimes. Lucy hurried away before he changed his mind.

Suzanne and Brad were at a table by themselves, sitting on the same side, their chairs close together. In their own world, Lucy thought. She went around to the empty side and put the shopping bag on the table.

Suzanne frowned at the bag, then at Lucy. Brad looked curious.

"Sorry to interrupt," Lucy said. Maybe that was why she didn't bother to try getting friendlier with Suzanne — she always made Lucy feel like an intruder. "I'll make this fast. Allen's mom gave me some of his stuff. She wanted his friends to have it, but she couldn't do it herself. So she asked me to, and here I am."

"How come she asked you?" Suzanne said.

Lucy shrugged. "I guess because we're neighbors. Were neighbors. And friends." What difference did it make?

Neither one of them made a move to look in the bag, so Lucy told them what was in it. "Oh, and there's a videotape, but I'm keeping that, at least for now."

"What's on it?" Brad asked. He put his arm around Suzanne, tightening his fingers on her shoulder.

Lucy described what she'd seen so far. "I haven't watched it all, but it's probably more of the same. I'll show you sometime if you want."

"No thanks," Suzanne said. "It would be horrible."

"Allen's not on it," Lucy reminded her. "He filmed it."

"I know that." Suzanne looked at Lucy, narrowing her blue eyes. "It would make me remember, though. It's different than a CD or a comic book. I'm surprised it didn't make you feel that way. I don't see how you can stand to look at it."

Oh, great. Now Lucy felt as if she'd come off cold and uncaring, even though she wasn't. "Well, everybody's different," she said quickly. She pulled out a box of baseball cards. "Brad? Do you want these?"

Brad shook his head. "I'll take the comic books, though."

Suzanne raised her eyebrows. "You don't still read them, do you?"

Brad's round face turned a little pink. "Sometimes," he admitted. "I have a lot because I used to collect."

Suzanne snorted. Lucy actually felt sorry for Brad. "I don't know how old they are," she said, pulling out the stack of comics and handing them to him.

"It doesn't matter." Brad put both his big hands over the comics, as if hiding them from his girlfriend. "That's not what this is about."

Lucy smiled at him. Maybe he wasn't as dense as she'd always thought. "Suzanne?" she said. "What about you?"

"No thanks." Suzanne picked up her container of yogurt. "I know this was Allen's mother's idea, but I really don't want anything. It gives me the creeps." She ate a spoonful of yogurt and snuggled against Brad.

Feeling as if she'd been dismissed, Lucy picked up the shopping bag and walked away.

When she passed Robert, his head was bent over his notes, and he didn't look up.

But all the way across the cafeteria, Lucy felt someone's eyes on her. Someone was watching her.

Chapter 3

The basketball was for Jon Eden. Not that shooting baskets with someone made you best friends, but Jon and Allen had played together, for a short time. Jon had to miss him.

Lucy wasn't sure Jon would want the basketball, but she thought he might like to be asked. And she was looking forward to doing the asking.

First she had to find him, though. By the time she did, school was over for the day. She'd given away the rest of the CDs to Dave Travis. He and Allen had hung out together sometimes. She'd given the remaining posters to Lindsey Baker, the girl Allen had taken to the junior prom, and a photo of Lindsey in her prom dress. She and Allen had only dated a few times that Lucy knew of, so it must not have been a great romance. But Lindsey was grateful and thanked her.

That left the baseball cards and the basketball.

Lucy had left her locker and was almost to the main doors when she spotted Jon up ahead of her. He was alone, walking fast. She ran to catch up with him, the bulky shopping bag rattling and banging against her leg.

Jon turned his head at the sound, and Lucy smiled at him, a bit nervous now that they were alone together.

"It was stupid to lug everything here," she said, slowing down to a walk. "If I'd been thinking, I would have asked everybody first and then brought it all in."

Jon stopped walking and smiled back. A small, tentative smile.

"Right, you don't know what I'm talking about," Lucy said. His eyes were gray, she noticed. Not that she'd gotten much chance to see them; he was looking at his watch now. "Are you in a hurry?"

"I have to get to work," he said. "But I've got a few minutes."

"Where do you work? Never mind," Lucy said quickly, feeling embarrassed that she was making a mess of their first real conversation. "I'll get to the point."

Jon waited, one eyebrow raised.

"Allen's mother wanted his friends to have some of his things," Lucy said. She described what Mrs. Torrance had given her, and told him what she'd kept and what she'd already given away. "I've got the baseball cards and the basketball left. I don't know why, but nobody seems to want the cards. You can have them, if you want. But mostly I thought you might like to have the basketball."

"Why?"

"Well, because you guys played together a lot," Lucy said. "I mean, I live right next door and I couldn't help seeing you, so I thought . . ." She stopped. "Look, you're in a hurry. Do you want it?"

Jon took the bag from her hand and pulled out the basketball. "Allen wasn't very good at this," he said, holding the ball in one hand. "Neither am I, though, so it was pretty even. We had fun." He bounced the basketball at his feet a couple of times. "Allen used to talk about you sometimes."

Lucy felt her face get hot. "Oh?"

Jon nodded. "He told me you're fun to tease."

"Allen thought everybody was fun to tease."

"Yeah. He said he surprised you with that video camera a few times," Jon said.

"Well, he surprised everybody with it," Lucy said. "I looked at his tape last night, though, and I didn't see myself in any embarrassing situations. Of course, I didn't look at all of it." She paused, knowing her face was really red now. "Well? Are you going to tell me what awful shots he got of me that I'm going to erase as soon as I get home?"

Jon laughed. Lucy realized it was the first time she'd seen him do that. She'd heard him, over at Allen's, but she'd never seen him. It made a big difference. His eyes, the color of the sky outside, looked much friendlier. "Oh, I get it," she said. "Allen told you I was easy to tease and you decided to find out."

"He was right."

"He didn't get any embarrassing film of me at all, did he?"

"You never know . . . ," Jon said with a sly grin. "You might want to destroy the tape, though, just in case."

Lucy returned the grin. "Okay, he was right. I'm easy to tease. Now, do you want the basketball?"

"Sure." Jon tucked it under one arm and they walked to the doors together. "Thanks for thinking of me, Lucy."

Outside, Jenny's weather prediction had

come true. It was pouring. Lucy set down her stuff and pulled up her hood. Even before she'd finished, her hair was drenched.

By the time she'd picked up her books and the bag, Jon was down the steps and halfway across the street. His head was bare, and his dark-blond hair was plastered to it. He didn't run, though. He walked steadily, Allen's basketball still under one arm.

Lucy watched him for a second. For a moment he'd warmed up a little, but mostly he'd kept a careful distance. As if he had some kind of secret he was trying to hide. Did he? she wondered.

But that was a stupid thing to wonder. Everybody had secrets.

Except maybe Allen.

By the time Lucy got home, the rain had let up. But she knew there was more to come. The wind was rising, and blowing dark, mean-looking clouds across the sky. As Lucy shut the front door behind her, thunder cracked like a rifle and made her jump.

The house was dark and full of shadows. Her parents wouldn't be home for at least two more hours. As Lucy walked down the hall, through the living room, and into the kitchen, she turned on a couple of lamps. But she opened the curtains and blinds so she could look out and watch the storm. She loved this kind of day.

And it was Friday, too. She had homework, but it could wait until later. Or tomorrow.

Roused from sleep, Moe padded softly into the kitchen and walked a figure eight between her feet, hoping for food. But another crack of thunder sent him racing from the room. She knew he'd spend the rest of the storm hiding under her bed.

Lucy was staring into the refrigerator when more thunder came. The lights flickered, but stayed on. Lucy loved this kind of day, except when the electricity went out.

Her mother had left a big note taped to the microwave: *Defrost chicken legs.* Lucy took them out of the freezer, put them in the microwave, and punched in the timing.

Then she got herself a soda and some leftover popcorn and went down the hall into her room.

A sharp rattling against her window made her turn and look out. Raindrops, driven by the wind, beat against the glass like bullets.

Across the yard, Allen's house was dark, the blinds and curtains closed. Remembering the light she thought she'd seen the night before, Lucy smiled. She wouldn't see it anymore. She'd taken care of his ghost today.

Lucy changed into sweatpants and a sweatshirt, munching popcorn and sipping soda while she did. She was on her way to the den when the lights flickered again. This time they went out.

Except for the wind and the rain rapping against the windows, the house was quiet. An eerie quiet, the way it got when the refrigerator didn't hum and the furnace didn't rumble.

Wondering how long this was supposed to last, Lucy went into the den. She had her hand on the television knob when she remembered there wasn't any electricity.

Candles, she thought. Before it got any darker and she couldn't see to light them.

There was one candle in the junk drawer in the kitchen, bent and burned halfway down. There had to be more somewhere.

The garage. Lucy remembered. Her father had bought a box of emergency candles and her mother said there was no place to keep them in the kitchen; put them in the garage.

There were two doors in the kitchen. One opened to the backyard, the other to the garage. Lucy pushed the door to the garage open and went down the two steps onto the concrete floor. She found the box of candles on the shelf above the worktable and was stretching for it when the phone rang.

Good. At least that was still working.

Her fingers were already closed around the box of candles, so Lucy yanked at it. As the phone rang a second time, the box came crashing down and twelve fat, white candles rolled from the worktable to the floor. Lucy stepped on at least three of them on her way to the kitchen.

The phone rang a third time.

Back in the kitchen, Lucy headed toward the other side of the room. Wearing only socks, she skidded and bumped her hip painfully against the table. The phone rang again.

"Okay, okay." Lucy finally made it across the room, rubbing her hip with one hand and grabbing the phone off the hook with the other.

A click.

Whoever was calling had hung up.

Lucy hung up, too, and went back into the garage to retrieve the candles. She'd smashed two of them, so she threw them away and took the rest back inside.

In her room, Lucy checked on the cat. From

under the bed, he widened his pale green eyes at her and hunched down, his tail wrapped around his paws. He wasn't going to budge until things got back to normal.

Lucy lit two candles, put one on her night table and one on her desk. The flames threw shadows onto the walls and made Lucy feel as if she was in a cave. It was spookier than without any light at all.

Just as Lucy blew out the first candle, the phone rang again. She should have stayed in the kitchen.

Blowing out the other candle, Lucy hurried out of the room and down the hall.

When she was at the kitchen door, the phone rang a second time. Lucy picked it up before it had a chance to ring again.

"Hello?"

Silence.

"Hello?" Lucy raised her voice a little. Maybe it was a bad connection.

More silence.

There was no crackling on the line. The connection was fine.

Lucy opened her mouth to say hello a third time, but suddenly she stopped, listening.

Someone was on the other end. She could

feel it. The silence wasn't empty. It was expectant, waiting.

The kitchen was darker now. The wind whistled outside, throwing sheets of rain against the house.

Lucy shivered at the sound. She wished the lights would come back on.

It was a prank call, probably. Or an obscene one. Or a burglar trying to find out if anybody was home. Whatever it was, it couldn't hurt her.

But just in case it *was* a bad connection without any crackling, Lucy said hello again.

A sigh came across the line, breaking the silence.

Chapter 4

Lucy was sure she hadn't imagined it. A whisper of breath, like a sigh.

Someone was on the other end of the line, waiting her out.

You win, Lucy thought, and was just about to put the receiver back when there was a click in her ear.

Whoever it was had hung up.

Five minutes later, after Lucy had checked to make sure the doors were locked, the lights came back on. From out in the hall, she heard the microwave start again, picking up where it had left off. The refrigerator started humming, and down in the basement, the furnace kicked in.

Then the phone rang.

Lucy felt better with the lights on. She turned from the front door and hurried into the kitchen, ready to shout at the unseen caller. It was probably just what the caller wanted, but she didn't care. She was mad. That sigh had been scary and she felt like yelling.

Grabbing the phone off the hook, Lucy took a big breath. "Listen, if you don't stop this, I'm calling the police," she said angrily. "I'm home, so you can't rob the place. And if this is a crank call or something, then you've got one chance to stop it or your next call will be to a lawyer. Do you get the picture?"

"I get it," a voice said.

Jon's voice. Jon Eden.

Lucy started to laugh, but then she stopped. "Was that you?" she asked.

"Umm . . ." Jon paused. "When?"

"Now," Lucy said. "I mean a few minutes ago." She shifted the phone to her other ear and leaned against the refrigerator. "What I mean is, did you call before?"

"No, but I take it somebody did," Jon said.

"Yeah." Lucy finally laughed. "Sorry about that. The lights went out and I got two calls. Nobody said anything, they just breathed in my ear. It scared me a little."

"Sounds pretty creepy," Jon agreed. "You really gave me an earful — too bad it wasn't the same caller this time."

"I'm glad it was you," Lucy said. "Well, anyway, the lights are back on and the phone's tied up, so they couldn't get through even if they wanted to."

"We lost our lights at the warehouse for a while, too," Jon said.

"Warehouse?"

"Where I work," he explained. "Three days a week after school, shipping out boxes of assemble-it-yourself furniture. Actually, I don't do the shipping. Mostly I shove the boxes from one place to another."

"Saving for college?" Lucy asked.

"Partly. Plus I'm trying to help out some," he said. "My dad's gone and the bills keep coming."

"Gone?" Lucy said. "You mean . . . is he . . . ?"

"Dead? No. I mean gone, as in divorce."

"Oh. That's too bad." Dumb thing to say, Lucy thought. Maybe it wasn't too bad. Maybe his father was a jerk. She cleared her throat. "Well . . ."

"Right, why did I call?" Jon said. "I called because I forgot to tell you something else Allen said about you."

"Oh, great, I'll bet he told you about my

bathrobe, didn't he?" Lucy said. "That I look like a blimp in it."

"No. Do you?"

Lucy laughed again. "I'm not answering. Just tell me what he said."

"He said if I asked you out, he thought you might go."

Maybe she shouldn't have been surprised. After all, he'd never called her before, and she didn't think he was the kind to call without a reason. But she *was* surprised. And excited.

"Lucy, are you there?" Jon asked.

"I'm here," Lucy said, straightening up. "I guess you're asking me for a date, huh?"

"That's what I'm doing."

"Okay. Well, sure," Lucy said. "I'd really like that."

"Great. Allen was right." Jon paused again, and Lucy could almost hear him smile. "How about tomorrow night?" he asked.

"Sure, tomorrow night's fine." Lucy was already thinking about what to wear. "What time? Where to?"

"I'll come by at six-thirty, quarter-to-seven. A movie and something to eat, okay?"

"Sounds great," Lucy said. "My parents aren't going to be happy, though. They'll already be gone to a party so they won't get to meet you."

"Check me out, you mean."

Lucy laughed. "Yes, that's exactly what I mean."

"Maybe another time," Jon said.

"Sure." I hope there is another time, Lucy thought. "Well, anyway, see you tomorrow."

"Right. And Lucy?"

"Yes?"

"If your silent caller calls again," Jon said, "don't tell him you're by yourself."

"What do you mean?" Lucy asked. "How do you know I'm here alone?"

"You told me," Jon said. "You said, 'I'm here, so you can't rob the place.' Next time, say 'we're here.' Or don't say anything at all. Just hang up."

In spite of herself, Lucy's eyes strayed to the back doors, to make sure they were locked. They were, but she shivered a little anyway. "Okay," she agreed. "Talk to you later."

By the time the phone rang again, Lucy's mother was home and the storm had passed. The cat had surfaced and gone outside, his tail high, as if he hadn't spent the last hour cringing under the bed.

It was Jenny calling, wanting to know if Lucy could go to the library with her the following night. "I can't go during the day, but I've got a paper due. I need somebody there to share the torture."

"I can't," Lucy said. "I've got a date."

A date wasn't that rare an occurrence, but Jenny shrieked anyway. "You're kidding! Who with?"

"Jon Eden," Lucy said, enjoying the sound of his name again.

"No! Really?"

"Really," Lucy said. She stretched the phone cord to the other side of the room so she could check on the chicken. "He called before, when the lights were out. Hey," she added, pulling open the oven door, "you didn't call, too, did you? I got these two creepy calls from a breather."

"Why would I call and breathe at you?" Jenny asked.

"I didn't mean that," Lucy laughed, closing the oven. "I meant maybe it was really a bad connection and I imagined the breathing."

"Maybe you did. But I didn't call until now,"

Jenny said. "Anyway, I hope you have fun tomorrow."

"Me too," Lucy said. "My mom's all mad because she wants to meet him but she and Dad are going out. I wonder what he's like. He's really cute, but there's something sort of . . . mysterious about him, you know?"

Jenny laughed. "Well, you're about to find out."

Jon wasn't cold. He wasn't even slightly cool. Not that he put any moves on her or anything, but he was talkative and joking and friendly. Lucy kept remembering the way he was before he'd called her yesterday.

What had made him change? Or had she just not given him a chance?

After the movie — a comedy about a case of mistaken identity — they drove to a hamburger place on Main Street.

"I want a cheeseburger," Lucy said as they slid into a booth. "And I'll pay for it."

Jon laughed. "Don't let what I said about my dad make you think we're desperate."

"I don't." Lucy shrugged off her jacket and stuffed it next to her on the seat. "I want to pay, that's all."

"Okay, I won't argue." Jon laughed again. "Allen warned me you were stubborn."

Lucy leaned her elbows on the table and cupped her chin in her hands. "Why don't you just tell me everything he said about me and get it over with?" she suggested. "That way, I won't have to keep wondering."

Jon grinned and shook his head. "I'm just teasing," he said. "I've told you everything."

Lucy didn't really believe him, but she decided to drop it. After they'd ordered their food, she asked him where he'd moved from and how he liked Bridgetown.

They'd moved from Jocelyn, a hundred miles away, Jon told her. "My mother works for a big electronics company. When it moved — well, it's about twenty miles from here — we did, too." Their Cokes came, and he took a sip. "I like it here okay," he went on. "I'll be going to college next year anyway, so it wouldn't matter much if I didn't like it. It's harder on my brother. He's in eighth grade now and he still talks about going home."

"Hey, does he like baseball cards?" Lucy asked. "I've still got Allen's.

"He's down on everything right now," Jon said. "When he lightens up I'll ask him."

Just then, Lucy saw Suzanne and Brad come in.

As they headed toward the back of the diner, Suzanne noticed Lucy. She stopped so quickly that Brad bumped into her from behind.

Lucy waved and, for a minute, she thought Suzanne was going to come to their table. She looked like she wanted to say something. Something not very pleasant.

Suzanne's eyes slid from Lucy to Jon, then back to Lucy. She raised an eyebrow, lifted her hand in an idle wave, and kept on walking.

"Friend of yours?" Jon asked jokingly.

Lucy nodded weakly. "She and Brad were really Allen's friends, though I still don't understand why. Allen was so outgoing and open, and they're not. At least, Suzanne isn't."

"Allen was a good guy," Jon agreed. "A 'live and let live' kind of person. It seemed like he got along with everyone."

Lucy thought about that for a minute. Had she ever seen Allen have a fight with anyone or heard him criticize somebody, except jokingly? She couldn't remember.

The waiter came with their burgers, and they were quiet for a few minutes, pouring ketchup and eating. Lucy had just taken a big bite when Jon broke into her thoughts. "Listen, I really hate to do this, but I have to leave."

"Leave?" Lucy said. "Why? What's wrong?"

"Nothing. You stay here and I'll be right back," Jon said, sliding out of the booth. "My mother talked my brother into going to his school's Spook Night. I dropped him off before I picked you up." He grinned. "I've got the car, and we only have one, so we made a deal — I'd run get him and drive him home. I'm really sorry. But I'll only be gone fifteen minutes."

"Well . . . but I can come if you want," Lucy said.

"No — we just got our food," Jon said, pulling on his jacket. He leaned over and pushed a lock of Lucy's hair off her forehead. "And we haven't finished talking. You stay here and eat. I won't be long."

Jon left quickly, his long legs getting him to the door in about three strides. Lucy settled back in the booth and took a bite of her cheeseburger. Jon's would be cold by the time he got back. Although she understood why he'd had to go, she still felt annoyed.

"Look," a voice said nearby. "You told me you'd take care of it."

Suzanne's voice. Full of anger and something else. Fear, maybe?

Lucy peered around the edge of the booth. Suzanne was on the phone, looking as mad as she sounded.

"You promised," Suzanne said into the phone. "If it doesn't work out, I'll think of something else. Just try!"

Suzanne slammed the phone onto its hook. Not wanting to be caught eavesdropping, Lucy turned around in her seat and picked up her burger.

Seconds later, a shadow fell across Lucy's table. "I saw your date leave," Suzanne said. "What happened?"

That's what bothered her the most, Lucy realized — she was afraid somebody would think Jon had walked out on her. "He had to pick up his little brother," she said.

Suzanne looked skeptical, but Lucy suddenly didn't care what anybody thought.

"Well, do you want to sit with Brad and me?" Suzanne asked, looking at her watch.

"Thanks, Suzanne, but Jon'll be back," Lucy said. "He really did go pick up his brother."

"So why don't you sit with us until he comes back?" Suzanne checked her watch again.

"What are you doing?" Lucy asked with a laugh. "Timing him?"

Suzanne dropped her arm to her side and bit her lip. "I just thought you might like some company, that's all." She shifted her weight to one foot and glanced around the diner. Her eyes stopped on the big clock above the counter.

It was ten after nine. Jon should be back in a few more minutes, Lucy thought.

Looking away from the clock, Lucy saw that Suzanne was watching her. Biting her lip again.

What was she so impatient about?

Or was it impatience? Suzanne's blue eyes didn't look annoyed.

They looked frightened.

Chapter 5

Jon came back at twenty-five after nine.

By that time, Suzanne had left Lucy's table and gone back to Brad. Lucy had asked her what was wrong, but Suzanne acted surprised and annoyed at the question. Nothing was wrong, she'd said. What made Lucy think anything was wrong?

Lucy decided to drop it. She knew something was the matter. But Suzanne obviously didn't want to talk about it; not to Lucy, anyway.

Waiting, Lucy finished her cheeseburger and her soda, and fidgeted with the straw. She was beginning to feel self-conscious again, when Jon appeared at the booth. His cheeks were ruddy and he smelled of the cold air outside. He slid into the seat across from her and took hold of her hand.

"I'm sorry," he said. "It took a few minutes

longer than I thought." He was a little breath-less, as if he'd been running.

"That's okay," Lucy said. Her annoyance disappeared as she realized how glad she was to see him, and how much she enjoyed his holding her hand. "Did he have fun?"

"What? Oh, Brian." Jon let go of her hand and picked up his hamburger, then set it back down without taking a bite. His eyes were dark-gray; he looked worried about some-thing, Lucy thought. Or maybe he was just bothered by the cold burger. "He probably did, but he wouldn't admit it."

Brian sounded like a pain, but Lucy decided not to say so. She suggested splitting an order of fries, and Jon agreed. When they came, he ate fast, like he had an appointment to keep.

Something had changed. He'd said he wanted to come back so they could talk some more. But Lucy was doing most of the talking. Jon just listened.

But was he listening? He kept checking the time, just like Suzanne.

What was going on, anyway? Everybody was acting as if they were in a big hurry.

Finally, Lucy gave up. Right in the middle of a sentence. "I applied to five colleges, but only . . ." she said, and stopped.

Jon didn't even notice.

"Hey," Lucy said sharply.

His eyes snapped up. "Sorry, what were you saying?"

"That it's time to go." Lucy wadded up her napkin and tossed it on the table. "Don't you think?"

Jon looked at his watch for about the tenth time.

"I have a curfew," Lucy said.

"Ten o'clock?"

"More or less." Actually more, but Lucy just wanted to go. She counted out her share of the money, then slid out of the booth and put on her jacket.

Jon stood by, watching. He looked disappointed. But he didn't argue, Lucy noticed.

The ride home was short. Lucy's house was only five minutes away.

It was a quiet ride, too. Jon said a few things, and Lucy answered, but she didn't keep the conversation going. She wasn't really angry, just confused.

Why had he changed so much when he came back? Did he have an argument with his brother? His mother? And why didn't he just say so, instead of clamming up?

She probably should have asked him, but

she didn't. Maybe she was angrier than she'd thought.

The porch light was on at Lucy's house, but her father's car was gone. Lucy could tell because the garage door was up and only her mother's car was inside. Lucy smiled.

"What?" Jon asked, noticing.

"I was just thinking about all the times my parents get after me to shut the garage door," she said. "They're the ones who forgot this time."

"Be sure to remind them," Jon said.

"Don't worry, I will." Lucy pushed open the car door and started to get out, but Jon put his hand on her arm.

"Lucy," he said. "Can we try again?"

"Try what?"

"Another date." He let go of her arm. "I promise not to leave in the middle of it."

"I wouldn't mind so much if you left," Lucy said, "as long as you didn't come back grumpy."

"Okay, it's a deal." Jon pushed her hair off her forehead again and smiled. "I'll walk you to the door."

"Thanks."

So. He didn't want to talk about whatever had happened when he left, Lucy thought.

She'd given him the chance, but he hadn't taken it.

Maybe next time. She'd sort of agreed to a next time.

Or maybe she should just forget it.

They said good night at the door and Jon went back to his car. Lucy heard it back out as she pushed open the door. Moe raced past her onto the porch, looking indignant at being shut in the house for so long.

Inside, Lucy took off her jacket and headed for the kitchen to get something to drink. She poured a glass of juice and was taking a sip when the red light on the answering machine caught her eye. There were two messages.

Punching the button, Lucy drank some more and waited.

The machine whirred and beeped. Then there was a click. The first caller had hung up.

More whirring. Then another click.

Another hang-up.

Slowly, Lucy lowered the glass and put it on the counter.

She thought about the calls from the day before.

She thought about the garage door. She couldn't even remember the last time her parents had left it open.

Lucy checked both doors in the kitchen. Both were locked.

But that didn't mean anything. If someone had come in one of the doors, they could have gone out one of them, locking it behind them.

Should she check the rest of the house or go to a neighbor's and wait until her parents came home?

Or was she getting scared over nothing?

If somebody was in the house now, they'd be looking to get out, right?

Lucy listened, straining her ears, trying to hear a noise or sense a presence. All she heard was her heart thudding.

"Okay," she said loudly. Her voice was shaky and so were her knees, but she walked out of the kitchen, making as much noise as she could in sneakers, and hurried down the hall to the front door.

The cat sauntered back in when she opened the door. Lucy made a grab for him, but he picked up his pace and trotted down the hall toward her room.

A cold wind had come up, blowing against Lucy as she stepped onto the front porch. She kept one hand on the doorknob, still not sure what she was going to do.

Tomorrow was Halloween. Maybe some

neighborhood kids were starting their tricks a day early.

But no way would she go into the dark garage to see if someone had sprayed shaving cream all over.

Shivering in the cold, Lucy saw headlights sweep around the corner at the end of the block. The car slowed as it neared the house.

Lucy's heartbeat slowed, too. It was her parents.

"You're home!" her mother said, getting out of the car. "How was your date?"

"Fine." Lucy kept her hand on the doorknob. "How was the party?"

"Nice." Mrs. Monroe frowned. "What are you doing standing out here in the cold?"

"I got scared," Lucy said. "There were two hang-up calls on the answering machine and the garage door was open. I was afraid maybe somebody called to make sure the house was empty and then broke in."

Her mother pushed open the door, peering over Lucy's shoulder into the hall. "Well, before you get too upset, let's ask your dad — maybe he left the garage door open," she said.

Mr. Monroe insisted he hadn't left the garage door up, but he didn't think anyone had broken in. Still, because Lucy seemed so shaken, he helped her check every room and closet. Except for the cat, nobody was lurking anywhere.

"Of course, if anybody *did* steal anything, you'd never know it," Mr. Monroe commented, looking around Lucy's room. "Maybe you should straighten up in here. Then you'd know if something was missing."

"Very funny," Lucy said. "I know exactly where everything is."

Still, after her father left to change his clothes, Lucy did an inventory. There was a pile of clothes on the chair, wobbly towers of books and stacks of papers on the desk, the night table, and the floor.

Nothing seemed to have been moved. And anyway, she didn't have anything valuable to steal.

Shaking off the creepy feeling, Lucy got into her bathrobe and went to take a shower. Her father had probably left the garage door up; he just wouldn't admit it. Whoever called had the wrong number, or didn't want to leave a message. No one had broken into the house.

Her imagination was working overtime, Lucy decided. Allen was dead. The next day was Halloween.

She had ghosts on her mind.

*   *   *

Even though Sunday was Halloween, the ghosts had disappeared. Except for the ones who trooped to the front door, demanding candy.

Lucy had spent most of the afternoon studying, taking half an hour out to call Jenny and tell her about the date with Jon.

"What's his problem?" Jenny asked, after Lucy had described his change of mood.

"I've decided it's a bratty little brother," Lucy said. "Brian — that's his brother's name — didn't want to move here, and it sounds like he's taking it out on everybody."

"So Jon took it out on you?" Jenny sounded indignant.

"I'm not sure about that anymore," Lucy said. "I think I made a bigger deal out of it than it was."

"Yeah, maybe. But he could have said something. And it's kind of weird, leaving you by yourself in the diner." Jenny paused. "So get to the good part. Did he kiss you good night?"

Lucy grinned. "Sorry. Maybe next time."

"He didn't?" Jenny's voice squeaked. "Lucy, I really think he's a dud!"

"Well, I didn't kiss him good night, either,"

Lucy laughed. "Does that mean I'm a dud, too?"

"Okay, never mind." Jenny sighed. "Anyway, you know the tape of Allen's? I've been thinking about it. I'm doing this project for video class and if his tape's any good, I could use it. Plus I thought if I edited it and put music to it, it might be a nice thing to give to his parents. Could I look at it?"

"Sure, but I want to see the rest of it first," Lucy said, remembering Jon's joke about Allen "catching" her on camera.

"Okay, so do it, and then let me have it," Jenny said.

After they hung up, Lucy studied some more. But from four o'clock on, it was impossible to concentrate because the trick-or-treaters kept the doorbell ringing.

Jenny handed out candy until about eight, then went into the den, rewound Allen's tape, and sat back to look at it.

The car wash, the party, the street scenes — Lucy watched it with one eye. It was kind of boring, but maybe Jenny could jazz it up with music. She'd have to cut a lot, though, because some of it seemed to go on forever.

Another party. Jenny sat up, frowning, trying to recognize the setting. The camera panned over smiling faces — Brad and Suzanne, Robert, Dave Travis, Jenny. Vicki and Diane, a couple of girls Lucy didn't know very well.

The camera stopped on a framed photograph, then zoomed in close. It was a photo of Robert, standing next to a blue car, holding up the keys and grinning. He'd gotten the car last year.

The party was at Robert's house, and now Lucy remembered — he'd given a party early in September. Lucy had been invited but she'd had to visit her grandmother that weekend.

Now the camera was back on the faces of the party-goers, and there was Jon. Lucy scooted to the edge of her chair.

He was sitting near the others, watching and listening, but not joining in the talk. Then he noticed the camera and held out a hand, as if to turn Allen away.

The camera stayed on Jon's face until he stood up and walked away. Then all Lucy saw was his back.

The picture got dark for a few seconds, and then suddenly Jon was facing the camera again. It looked as if he was in a hallway or something.

There was a door behind him, and no one else seemed to be around, except Allen.

The camera zoomed up close on Jon's face, and Lucy would have enoyed it, except for his expression: Jon was furious.

His mouth moved, and he was talking, saying something in anger. His gray eyes were dark, Lucy noticed, the way they'd been the night before.

Allen kept the camera rolling, recording it all.

Then Jon moved, walking quickly toward the camera with his hand out. His hand filled the lens until all Lucy could see was darkness.

Chapter 6

Lucy picked up the remote control and stopped the tape.

She felt funny, as if she'd seen something she shouldn't have. Something private.

What had happened after Jon put his hand over the lens? Had he knocked the camera to the floor?. Knocked Allen to the floor? He'd looked mad enough to do it. But why?

She tapped her palm with the remote control. She could look some more, but the tape wouldn't tell her what the argument was about. She'd never really know unless she asked, and she wasn't sure about doing that. The argument was in the past. Maybe it should stay there.

But Jon's face — eyes narrowed in anger, lips twisted when he talked — Lucy couldn't forget it. What had Allen said or done to make him so mad?

Had she seen Jon at Allen's playing basketball after that party? She couldn't remember — the days blurred together in her mind.

One thing for sure — she'd have to tell Jenny to cut out that part of the tape. Except, it didn't seem right to let *anyone* see it.

So she'd erase it herself. That was easy enough. She could get it out of sight, at least.

Lucy punched the rewind button, listened to the VCR whir, then stopped it. The shot of Robert and his car — she'd gone too far back.

She punched fast-forward and waited for the machine to get going. It whirred for a second, then clunked to a stop.

Lucy pressed play. Nothing happened.

She pressed rewind. Nothing. Then fast-forward. The VCR whined, but the tape didn't move.

Getting up, Lucy tried the buttons on the VCR itself, but she couldn't get it to do anything. The machine was broken.

Good. She didn't want to watch that ugly scene again, anyway. Not even to erase it.

"I don't see what the big deal is," Jenny said the next morning at school. "I know Allen's dead, and I really miss him, but face it —

somebody was going to knock that camera out of his hand sooner or later."

"I didn't say he knocked it out of his hand," Lucy said. "I was just guessing." Lucy had decided after all to tell Jenny about Jon's scene on the tape. Except it wasn't just a "scene," she kept remembering. It was real.

"Well, whatever." Jenny pulled open the door and they joined the stream of students in the hallway. "Allen got carried away with that stupid camera and it was starting to get annoying. Jon was probably in a bad mood, and Allen just made it worse."

Lucy looked at Jenny as they turned a corner, heading for the lockers. "Well, you were there," she reminded her. "At Robert's party. Was Jon in a bad mood?"

Jenny thought for a moment, then shrugged. "I can't remember," she said. "If he was, I didn't notice. He was kind of quiet, I remember that. But he was new. He didn't know anybody very well."

"What about Allen?" Lucy asked. "When he came back inside, from the hall or whatever, did he look upset? And did Jon leave early, or did he come back?"

Jenny shook her head. "Lucy, I didn't spend the whole night watching them, all right?" she said. "I think you're making too much out of it."

"Maybe you're right," Lucy said. "But I wish I hadn't seen it. It changes things."

"How?" Jenny asked. "Everybody gets mad sometimes and loses their temper. Just because Allen recorded it doesn't make Jon some kind of monster. He's probably forgotten all about it. You're just embarrassed because you saw it."

"I guess that's it," Lucy agreed. "I'll try to forget it."

"Good," Jenny said. "Give me the tape and I'll show you how to use the equipment in the lab and you can erase it yourself. Then nobody else'll ever see it. And don't mention it to Jon, either, or your second date might be your last."

"Okay." Lucy laughed, and then stopped when she opened her locker. Three notebooks and a sheaf of looseleaf paper slipped out and landed at her feet. "Hey."

"What?" Jenny asked.

"My locker's all messed up," Lucy said, picking up the notebooks. "Nothing's where I left it. Look," she added, pulling out a baseball cap, "This was on a hook and now it's on the bottom of the locker."

Jenny laughed. "You actually remember where the stuff in your locker was?"

"I do when it's all been moved around," Lucy said. "I wonder if somebody's been in here." She took off the combination lock and turned it over in her hands. "It hasn't been broken," she said. "Do you think somebody figured out the combination? Or wait — maybe they looked it up." The locks and their combinations were issued by the school office at the beginning of the year, and the office kept a record of them. "Why would somebody break into my locker?"

"I don't know." Jenny shifted her books from one arm to the other. "Did you keep any money in there?"

"No, but this is really weird," Lucy said. "I wonder if it happened to anybody else."

"Let's ask." Jenny reached out and grabbed the arm of someone passing by. It happened to be Robert. "Lucy thinks somebody went through her locker," she said. "What about yours?"

Robert peered curiously into Lucy's locker. "Huh," he said. "Was anything stolen?"

"I don't think so. I didn't have anything valuable in here, anyway," Lucy said. "But that's not the point."

"I guess not." Robert straightened up. "Well, my locker's fine. Listen, I have to hurry — I've got a meeting with a college rep. Maybe you should report it, Lucy," he added as he walked away.

"He's right," Jenny said. "Tell the office. Demand a new lock."

Lucy nodded. "I will. And check your locker, too."

Jenny laughed. "The only way I'd know someone's been in it is if they cleaned it up. But I'll take a look."

Jenny left then, to go to her own locker and then to homeroom.

Lucy put her jacket and the spilled papers away, thinking. Was someone looking for money, going through a lot of lockers, trying to find cash?

Or was it just *her* locker?

No, it couldn't have been. She didn't have anything worth stealing.

Shaking off the feeling of annoyance, Lucy shut her locker and started toward her own homeroom. When she turned the corner, she came face to face with Jon.

"Lucy, hi," he said, breaking into a smile.

For a second, his angry face on the videotape came into Lucy's mind. She blinked it away and smiled back at him. "Hi."

"What's wrong?" he asked, turning around and walking along with her. "You look worried. Got a test? Didn't do your homework?"

Lucy glanced up at him. He was grinning now, but she could still see that angry image of him from the tape.

"Hey," he said, slowing down and stopping. "What's up?" The grin was fading; he looked curious.

Lucy stopped, too. "Sorry," she said, forcing the image away again. She tried to think of some excuse and then remembered she had a perfectly good one: "Somebody broke into my locker."

It wasn't a tragedy, and Lucy didn't expect him to treat it that way. But she never expected the reaction she got.

Jon's look of curiosity disappeared; his jaw tightened, his eyes darkened, and a faint blush swept over his lean face.

He wasn't embarrassed, though. He was angry.

Not the same anger as the face on the tape. Not as intense. But close enough to make Lucy take a step back.

Make a joke out of it, she told herself. Don't ask him what's wrong — he won't tell you. "Hey," she said, as lightly as she could manage. "There's good news, too. Nothing was taken. Anyway, I've got to get to homeroom. Talk to you later, okay?"

A quick smile, and Lucy was gone.

But until she turned another corner, she felt Jon's eyes on her back.

No one else's locker had been broken into. Lucy found that out at lunchtime, which she'd cut short so she could go to the office and get a new lock. She had to turn in her old lock and fill out a form. The woman behind the desk couldn't find the forms. "Yours is the first new lock we've issued this semester," she said, pulling open the third file drawer. "Are you sure about what happened?"

Lucy looked impatiently at the clock. If she didn't hurry, she'd be late for history. "Yes, I'm sure," she said.

"Ah, here they are," the woman said, pulling some papers from the drawer. "Fill it out and then I'll give you a new lock. And I'll file the report, in case we start to get a pattern of break-ins."

Lucy was filling out the form, writing fast, when she heard the office door open behind her.

"Oh, good, it's you, Suzanne," the woman behind the desk said.

Lucy glanced behind her and saw Suzanne Gold.

Suzanne gave her a curious glance as she walked behind the counter.

"I'm going to rush out right now and return that coffeepot I bought yesterday," the woman said to Suzanne. "There's some typing in this basket; you can start after you take this girl's report." She put on her coat, lifted a large box from the floor, and hurried out of the office.

"What report's she talking about?" Suzanne asked, leaning her elbows on the counter in front of Lucy.

"Locker," Lucy said, signing her name. "Somebody broke into mine, so I came for a new lock."

"Broke into it?" Suzanne asked. "How? With a crowbar or something?"

Lucy shook her head. "No, they used my combination."

"What did they take?"

"Nothing. At least, I don't think they did." Lucy reached into her bag, pulled out her old lock, and set it on the counter with the form.

Suzanne disappeared into an inner room for a moment, then came back carrying a plastic bag with a new lock inside. "There," she said, setting it on the counter. "The combination's on that piece of paper taped to the lock. Memorize it and throw it away."

"I did that with the first one," Lucy said. "It didn't do me much good. And you keep a list of combinations in the office, don't you?"

Suzanne leaned on the counter again. "What do you mean?"

"I mean — "

"You mean you think I — or somebody else who works in here — was after something of yours?" Suzanne asked coldly. "Is that what you're saying?" She picked up Lucy's old lock and the form and turned away. Then she immediately turned back. "Why would I want anything of yours, Lucy? What makes you think that?"

"Nothing!" Lucy said. What was going on, anyway? "I just meant — "

"I know what you meant," Suzanne said, interrupting again. "You think I did it. Well, I didn't. If I wanted something, I wouldn't break into your locker to get it. How would I know it would be there?"

"How would you know *what* would be there?" Lucy asked. "I don't know what you're talking about, Suzanne!"

Lips pressed together, Suzanne took a deep breath and let it out slowly. "Okay, forget it." She breathed deeply again. "Okay?"

"Sure." Lucy picked up the new lock and left, before Suzanne erupted again.

As she hurried to history, Lucy tried to do what she'd said she'd do — forget it.

But she couldn't.

Suzanne worked in the office. Lucy had forgotten that. She worked there an hour a day, in place of study hall.

She could see the locker combinations any time she wanted to.

And she'd blown up over an innocent remark, as if she felt guilty.

As if she had something to hide.

Chapter 7

AP History was the only advanced placement course Lucy was taking, and it was hard. If she didn't concentrate, she'd miss something important. That day she missed a lot.

At least Robert was in the same class, she thought, glancing over at him. He never missed a thing. And he'd agreed to copy his notes for her, so she decided it was safe to let her mind wander that day.

It was impossible not to let it wander, anyway. When she'd first sat down, she was still thinking about Suzanne and her strange reaction about Lucy's locker.

Lucy tried to convince herself that Suzanne was just in a touchy mood. No, not touchy. A foul mood, that's what it was.

Suzanne had been that way for a few days now. Maybe she was having trouble with Brad, or trouble at home, and she wasn't thinking straight. If she'd been thinking straight, she would have realized that Lucy hadn't accused her of anything.

A terrible mood, that had to be it, Lucy thought.

But what about Jon? What was his excuse? Why had he looked so angry, angry enough to scare her?

Something at home? His mother? His brother? Maybe his dad was causing problems, not sending money or something.

But that didn't have anything to do with Lucy's locker. And it was when she talked about her locker that his face had changed.

Jon's face. Red with anger, just like on the tape.

The teacher, Mr. Shay, was pacing back and forth in front of his desk now, talking about the Constitutional Congress. Lucy tried to pay attention — she liked his enthusiasm, and usually she got caught up in it.

But her mind shifted to Jon again, and the teacher's words faded into the background.

She didn't really know him, Lucy thought. Would she ever know him? Did she want to?

Yes, she decided, she did want to. When he'd asked her out, she'd felt a lift, the way she felt after finishing a hard paper, or seeing sunshine after a week of cloudy days.

Cloudy days — that's what she'd been having since Allen died. And Jon felt like sunshine.

Or he had at first.

But she couldn't turn him off just because he'd gotten mad for some unknown reason. It wasn't fair.

Besides, she really wanted to know him better.

But when she did, would she like him?

"Ms. Monroe," a voice broke into Lucy's thoughts. "I have the feeling you're riding a different train of thought today than the rest of us."

It was Mr. Shay. Lucy felt her face get hot as some of the kids smiled.

Mr. Shay leaned on her desk. His eyes were friendly. "Are you feeling all right?"

Better to tell the truth, Lucy thought. "I'm fine," she said. "I'm sorry. I just can't concentrate."

"You mean I'm not being my usual scintillating self?" The teacher smiled and moved away, not expecting an answer. Lucy was off the hook.

After class, Robert walked out the door with

her. "I guess I'd better copy my notes from today, too," he said seriously. To him, any lapse in concentration was a catastrophe. "Where was your mind, anyway?"

"Just thinking about other things," Lucy said. "And yes, I'll need today's notes, too. Thanks, Robert."

"No problem." He started to walk on, but then caught himself. "Oh, hey, Lucy, I was supposed to give this to Jenny." He reached into his book bag and pulled out a thick folder. "It's a script we've been working on in video. Could you give it to her? I would have given it to her myself in the lab after school, but I have a dentist appointment and I have to leave early."

"Sure." Lucy took the folder and tucked it under her arm with her books.

"Great," Robert said. "And make sure she doesn't lose it. I don't want to type it over again."

Lucy promised to personally deliver it, then went off to her next class.

Jon was on her mind for the rest of the day, so when Lucy actually saw him after school, she felt embarrassed. Would her thoughts show on her face?

But if Jon noticed that she was uncomfortable, he didn't say anything. And he seemed back to normal, or at least, back to the way he'd been when he'd called to ask her out — friendly and teasing, almost flirty.

But before he'd called her, he'd been quiet. Cool and distant, Lucy remembered. Would the real Jon Eden please stand up?

"I forgot to tell you something," he said, catching up to her in the hall as she was heading to the video lab.

"About what?" Lucy was still thinking about his bad mood; maybe he was going to explain it.

"I've got wheels today," Jon said, putting his hand on her shoulder. "My mom took the day off. So . . ."

Lucy smiled. "So?"

He squeezed her shoulder. "So why don't I drive you home before I go to work?"

"Oh."

"Hey, it's just a ride," Jon said. "You don't have to sound that excited."

Lucy shook her head — she'd still been thinking about his "other" personalities. Laughing, she said, "No, a ride would be great." She tapped the folder Robert had given her. "But I have to give something to Jenny.

It'll just take a minute. You know Jenny Berger, don't you?" she asked as they walked to the video lab together.

"Sure. Not very well, though."

"Robert had a party in September," Lucy said. "I think Jenny said you were there." Lucy glanced at Jon out of the corner of her eye, wondering if he'd mention the argument with Allen that she'd seen on the tape.

But a crowd of kids came around the corner just then, laughing loudly and tossing a ball back and forth. Jon and Lucy got separated in the shuffle, and by the time they were back together, whatever reaction Jon might have had was gone.

Lucy decided not to mention the party again. If he wanted to say anything, he would. Anyway, Jenny was probably right — he'd most likely forgotten about it.

When they reached the video lab, Jenny wasn't there. No one was. "Weird," Lucy said. "This place usually has a few people in it at least."

Jon looked around at the recorders and monitors, the metal shelves holding other equipment, the thick cables snaking around the edges of the room. "Are you into this stuff, too?"

Shaking her head, Lucy walked to one of the tables and leaned against it. "Knowing how Robert is, I figure I'd better hand-deliver this," she said, pulling the folder he'd given her out of her duffel bag. "It's a script. Probably a prizewinner."

Jon checked the time, which was easy, since there were clocks all over the place — a big round one on the wall, plus digital ones on just about every recorder.

"I figured Jenny'd be here," Lucy said. "I would have given it to her before, but I didn't see her."

"I've got a few minutes," Jon said.

But a few minutes went by, and Jenny still hadn't come.

"Look, you have to go," Lucy said.

"Yeah, I do. Sorry." Stepping close to her, Jon tilted his head and smiled. He looked like he might kiss her but, just then, Suzanne rushed into the room. When she saw them, she came to a stop and said, "Oh."

Jon looked at her, frowning a little. Then he looked back at Lucy and smiled. "Another time, okay?"

"Okay." Lucy wondered if he was talking about a ride or a kiss. She'd have to wait to find out. "See you tomorrow."

"Sorry about that," Suzanne said to Lucy after Jon was gone. "I didn't know he'd be here."

"But you knew *I'd* be here?" Lucy hauled her duffel bag off the floor and looked through it, to make sure she'd put her English notebook in it.

Suzanne moved a little closer to Lucy. "I, um, I was looking for you."

Lucy glanced up. Suzanne was eyeing her duffel bag, frowning at it. "I know, it's falling apart," Lucy laughed, sticking her finger through a tear in it. "Oh, good, there's the notebook." She zipped the bag and put it back down on the floor. "How come you were looking for me?"

Suzanne bit her lip nervously. Then she said, "I just wanted to say I was sorry. About what happened in the office. I was kind of rotten about everything."

"Oh. Well, that's okay, Suzanne," Lucy said. She was a little surprised — did Suzanne actually give up some time with Brad to come and apologize? But Lucy was glad she had.

"Good. Well." Suzanne looked at the wall clock. "Thanks, Lucy. See you." As if she'd gotten something unpleasant over with, she turned and hurried out of the room as fast as she'd come in.

Alone again, Lucy walked around the room, getting impatient.

Where was Jenny? Where was anybody?

She figured she could just leave the script for Jenny with a note. But if anything happened to it, Robert would kill her. Lucy went to the door and looked up and down the hall. She could hear voices in other halls, and footsteps, but none of the footsteps were heading her way.

Jenny was probably on her way right now. Lucy decided to go intercept her. Letting the door to the video lab swing shut behind her, she walked down the hall and around the corner.

At the other end of the hall, past the video room, another door opened, and someone looked out. Lucy was walking away, and now she was out of sight.

When Lucy left the video room, it was empty. It would be empty when she came back. But for a few hurried, frantic moments in between, someone else would be there.

*　　*　　*

When she turned the corner, Lucy spotted a water fountain and got a drink. Someone passed by as she was bending over the fountain. She saw sneakered feet. Giant sneakered feet. Not Jenny.

Straightening up, Lucy wandered over to a bulletin board and read some notices about the school play, the computer club, and the junior class election. She glanced down the hall again. Jenny had to be coming from that direction, that's where her locker was.

No Jenny.

Just before she turned away from the bulletin board, another notice caught Lucy's eye. It was about a television producer who was going to speak in the auditorium. After school, that day.

That explained it. Jenny and every other video nut in the school were probably in the auditorium right now.

Sighing, Lucy headed back to the video lab. She'd peek into the auditorium, and if she saw Jenny, she'd give her the script. If she didn't, then it would just have to wait. It couldn't be so earthshakingly important that one night would make any difference.

At the lab, Lucy pushed open the door and went inside.

It was still empty, but now she knew why.

Halfway into the room, Lucy stopped. Everything seemed the same.

But something felt different.

She glanced around the room. The clocks and timers were all still clicking the seconds away. The cables and wires snaked across the floor. The monitors were all off, their screens staring back at her like blank, black eyes.

But there was something. . . .

The skin on the back of her neck prickled, and Lucy quickly looked over her shoulder. Nobody was lurking behind the door.

Giving herself a shake, Lucy walked over to the table where she'd left the folder.

She was just about to put it in her duffel bag when she realized what was different.

Her bag was on the table. But she'd left it on the floor.

Quickly, Lucy unzipped her bag and looked inside. She saw notebooks, books, pens, a pencil, an apple. Hairbrush, Kleenex, house keys, rubber bands, crumbs. And three dollar bills.

That was all the money she'd brought that day. No one had taken it.

But while she was gone from the room, someone had come in and pawed through her bag.

She'd been stupid to leave it here, but at least nothing had been taken. Grabbing the folder, Lucy slung her bag over one shoulder and started for the door.

Then she stopped, feeling that prickling on her skin again as she suddenly thought of something.

They hadn't taken her money. So what else could they have been after?

Chapter 8

A half hour later, Jenny found Lucy sitting on the floor across from the auditorium doors, her back against the wall, watching the kids file out.

"What are you doing here?" Jenny asked.

"Waiting for you." Lucy gathered her stuff and stood up. "Robert asked me to give you this," she said, holding out the folder.

Jenny opened it up and glanced inside. "Oh. His script," she sighed. "I wish he'd forget it. It's a great idea, but I don't want to 'collaborate' with him. I have my own ideas." She shut the folder and looked at Lucy. "You didn't have to wait out here to give it to me, but thanks. Are you walking home?"

"I guess I have to," Lucy said. "Jon offered me a ride, but then he couldn't wait any longer."

"Jon?" Jenny's eyes lit up. "I guess that means he's still interested."

"I guess." Lucy didn't feel like talking about Jon at the moment. She was still upset about what had happened to her duffel bag. "I figured you'd be in the lab after school," she said as they went down the hall. "I went there first."

"Yeah, I was going to be there, until I remembered the lecture," Jenny said.

Lucy nodded, pushed open the door, and they went out into the cold air. It was four o'clock and starting to get dark. Cars already had their headlights on.

"I waited in the lab for a few minutes, and then I went to look for you," Lucy said. "I saw a notice about the lecture on a bulletin board, so I knew where to find you." She shivered, not just from the cold. "I left my bag in there when I went down the hall, and somebody went through it."

"Really? Did they take anything?"

Lucy shook her head. "And I had money in it, too. Not much, but they left it."

"Well, that's good." Jenny pulled some mittens out of her pocket and put them on. "It's weird, isn't it? First your locker, then your bag."

Lucy shivered again. "That's what I was

thinking. It's not only weird, it's a little scary."

"What do you mean? It's just bad luck." Jenny frowned at the expression on Lucy's face. "Isn't it?"

"Maybe, maybe not," Lucy said slowly. "Remember the hang-up phone calls I told you about?"

Jenny nodded.

"When Jon took me home Saturday night, I thought somebody might have been in the house. Then my locker gets broken into," Lucy said. "Then somebody goes through my duffel bag. Nothing bad has really happened, though. Nobody's hurt and nothing's been stolen. It's as if somebody's trying to scare me."

Jenny frowned again. "But why?"

"I don't know," Lucy admitted. "But you read about stuff like this all the time. Stalkers."

"*Stalkers?*" Jenny looked skeptical. "I think you're imagining things. I mean, why would anybody stalk you?"

"Why would anybody stalk anybody?" Lucy asked. "They don't have reasons, not good ones. We're not talking about normal people, you know."

"Yeah, I guess so." Jenny still sounded doubtful. "It could still be a bunch of coincidences, though."

"Just a coincidence that only *my* locker was broken into?" Lucy asked.

"How do you know that?"

"The lady in the office told me when I went to get my new lock."

"Well, but yours can't be the only bag that's ever been gone through," Jenny pointed out. "And everybody's gotten hang-up calls."

"I know, I know," Lucy agreed. "It's just strange that all these things are happening at once. And that they didn't take anything from the bag or the locker. It's like they did it just for fun. Weird fun." She shivered again. "It scares me."

They'd reached the street corner where getting home took them in different directions. Jenny stopped walking. "What are you going to do?" she asked.

"I don't know," Lucy said. "I mean, I could be wrong. I hope I am. But if I'm right, I'm going to watch out."

Watch out. As Lucy left Jenny and headed home in the darkening afternoon, she wondered how she could possibly watch out for someone she'd never seen. *If* there was someone deliberately trying to scare her, that is.

Maybe she was just scaring herself. Maybe

Jenny was right, and everything that had happened was a coincidence.

A car swept by, spewing up water from the gutter. Lucy jumped aside, but a spray of dirty water splattered her sleeve. She turned around to give the driver a dirty look, saw the headlights of another car coming from behind, and moved to the inside edge of the sidewalk.

But the car didn't pass her. Lucy glanced over her shoulder and saw its headlights. The car was almost a full block behind her, moving slowly. Very slowly.

At the end of the block, Lucy turned the corner and looked back. The car was still there, moving slowly and steadily.

Lucy picked up her pace. Halfway down the block, when she saw the car's headlights sweep around the corner after her, she began to run.

She didn't stop running until she got to her house, around another corner and two long blocks away. Heart pounding, mouth dry, she raced up onto the porch, fumbled for her keys, and let herself inside, slamming the door behind her.

Almost immediately, she eased open the door and peered back out. A few cars drove by. One of them was a dark color, like the one that had cruised along behind her. But she couldn't really tell if it was the same one.

She couldn't tell if the car had really been following her, either, Lucy thought. It seemed like it had, but she'd just been talking about being stalked. Jenny would say it was a coincidence, or her imagination. Lucy wasn't so sure.

Her breathing was almost back to normal when something brushed against her leg and she jumped away, gasping.

Just the cat, wanting to go out.

Lucy pulled the door open a little wider and he slipped through, ears twitching at the outdoor sounds.

Locking the door, Lucy kicked off her shoes, left her coat in the hall, and went into the kitchen.

There was a message from her mother on the answering machine — she wouldn't be home until about seven-thirty, Lucy's father would be even later, and Lucy should do a load of laundry.

Lucy made herself a peanut butter sandwich and then called Jenny to tell her about the car. The line was busy. Lucy ate the sandwich while she watched TV. After a little while she tried Jenny again. Still busy.

Jenny would probably laugh, anyway. But maybe that's what Lucy needed. When Lucy called again a few minutes later, there was no answer.

Lucy went upstairs, emptied the hamper, and carried the dirty clothes downstairs to the laundry room. She'd just started the washing machine when she thought she heard the phone. She ran back upstairs, reaching the kitchen in time to hear the answering machine click off.

Lucy listened for the message, but the caller hadn't left one.

It's nothing, she told herself. Don't start getting spooked again.

The back door rattled, and Lucy felt her heart speed up. It rattled again, and she let her breath out. She recognized the sound — Moe had hooked his claws under the bottom of the storm door and pulled. It was his way of knocking.

With the cat inside and the doors locked, Lucy took her duffel bag into her room. Across the yard, Allen's house was dark and deserted-looking.

Lucy pulled down the shades, stretched out across the bed, and tried to read a few chapters in her English book. But her eyelids felt *so* heavy. . . . Finally she gave in, turned out the light, and fell into a light doze.

She dreamed of sounds. The thud of the basketball, a click on the phone line, the swish of car tires on the street. She knew she was dreaming, but the sounds seemed so real that she'd jolt awake every few seconds.

Then she'd feel the nubbly bedspread under her cheek, and hear the cat purring next to her ear. She'd turn her head and drift back to sleep.

She dreamed of voices, too. Someone shouted. She couldn't understand the words, but she knew it was Allen's voice. She heard Suzanne saying she was sorry, and Jenny and Robert talking about collaboration. She heard the words *watch out*, and jerked awake for a second. That had been Jon's voice.

She felt heavy, as if she were sinking into the mattress. She knew where she was, knew she was dreaming, but she couldn't make herself move enough to wake up completely. The voices and sounds all merged together, and Lucy tried to follow what was happening, but it was too confusing. She shut it out and sank deeper into sleep.

When Lucy came fully awake, the room was dark. She was stiff, as if she'd held her muscles tense the whole time. She squinted at the bed-side clock: six-fifteen. She'd been asleep for forty-five minutes.

Moe was hunched on the pillow near her head, his paws tucked under him. When he saw that she was awake, he started purring again.

But Lucy heard another sound, too.

What was it?

Resting her chin on her hands, she listened. The cat shifted, watching her. Then his eyes widened and his ears swiveled around, toward the side window.

Moe heard it, too.

A crisp, crunchy sound, like someone eating potato chips. Or walking on them.

Or someone walking cautiously across the winter-dried grass outside.

Chapter 9

Lucy pulled herself to her knees and listened some more.

Silence.

Maybe a dog, she thought. But dogs never walked carefully, they crashed around like bulldozers. Maybe it was another cat.

Her own cat stood up and stretched, then curled into a ball and went back to sleep.

Lucy scooted backward off the bed and walked to the side window. Pulling the shade back with her fingertip, she looked outside.

Just as dark out there as it was in her room.

Enough darkness. Leaving the window, Lucy went around to the other side of the bed. She was just about to snap on her lamp when she heard the noise again.

Her hand froze on the lamp switch and she listened in the dark.

Definitely not a dog. And too heavy for a

cat. A racoon was a slight possibility, but Lucy didn't believe it. Not after the phone calls, and the car, and her locker and bag.

Somebody was outside, in the yard. Crunching leaves and twigs and grass underfoot, trying to be quiet.

Trying to scare her.

Doing a good job of it.

Lucy's heart was thudding and her face felt hot. It wasn't all fear, though. Down deep, behind the fear, she felt a spark of anger.

The spark grew as she left her room and headed down the hall. She ought to be able to be alone in her own house without getting frightened. She shouldn't be harassed by phone calls and followed and have her things broken into.

As she passed the kitchen, she glanced in. Both doors were locked. She went to the front door, saw that it was still locked, and slid the safety chain into place. In the living room, she turned off the light so she couldn't be seen from outside, then started to go back to the kitchen.

She thought she heard the sound again, on this side of the house now. Standing in the middle of the living room, Lucy listened to make sure.

Yes, there it was. Outside the living room window.

Whirling around, Lucy ran out, down the hall and back toward the kitchen. She was going to call the police. She'd tell them not to use their siren. She wanted whoever was out there to be surprised. She hoped the police would turn a spotlight on the house, trapping the stalker in its glare. Scaring him to death the way he was scaring her.

But she had to hurry, or he might be gone, and she wanted him caught and stopped.

Just as Lucy grabbed the phone off the hook, the doorbell rang, startling her so badly she dropped the receiver. It banged against the wall and started swinging wildly back and forth.

The doorbell rang again.

Did he really expect her to come to the door?

Lucy caught the swinging phone, brought it to her ear, and was just about to punch the numbers when she heard a voice.

"Hello? Anybody home?"

Slowly, Lucy took her hand away. She knew that voice. She'd heard it in her dream earlier. She heard it almost every day at school. It was Robert's voice.

"Lucy?" she heard him call out. Then he

said something else, but more softly, and she didn't catch it.

Lucy hung up and ran to the front door. Switching on the porch light, she opened the door a crack, leaving the chain hooked.

Robert turned around. "Oh, hi. Lucy?"

"Just a second." She shut the door, slid the chain off, and pulled the door open wide. "Robert, come on in."

"I thought somebody was home," he said, stepping inside. "I mean, I saw a light go off when I was walking up."

"That was me," Lucy said. She looked out the door, but no one else was there, of course. Her stalker was long gone.

"You always shut your lights off at six-thirty?"

"There was somebody outside." Lucy shut the door and locked it again.

Robert looked at her as if her IQ level had just dropped several points. "I know," he said. "I was."

Lucy shook her head impatiently. "Not you. Somebody else was out there. I heard them, a long time before you came to the door. Did you see anyone?"

"No," he said. "You want me to go back out and take a look?"

"No, he's gone by now," Lucy said.

Robert looked concerned. "Who, Lucy?"

"Don't ask me," she said. "Some creep's been trying to scare me, that's all I know." She led the way into the den, Robert following. "I was just about to call the police when I heard you at the door," she said over her shoulder.

"That would have been exciting," Robert joked. " 'I'm innocent, officer. All I was doing was bringing her some notes.' "

"I would have vouched for you." Lucy laughed, feeling a little better. "Anyway, is that why you came — to bring me the history notes?"

Robert nodded and held out a bunch of stapled-together papers. "Test day after tomorrow, remember?"

"I guess I didn't hear that," Lucy said, thinking of how preoccupied she'd been in class. She took the notes and riffled through them. "Thanks, Robert, this is great. Oh, and I gave the script to Jenny, just so you know."

"Good, thanks."

Robert smiled and took a step toward the doorway.

He probably wanted to go home and study so he could get an A + instead of an A, Lucy thought. But she didn't want him to leave. Maybe if she talked long enough, she could keep him there until somebody got home.

"Listen," she said, "I feel like I should pay you back for the notes. Do you want something to drink? Or eat?" She glanced around the room. "How about watching television? Or a movie? Oh, no, we can't do that — the VCR's broken and we haven't even taken it in to be fixed yet."

"Uh, Lucy — "

"It broke right in the middle of Allen's tape," she went on. "Remember, I told you about it? But as soon as I can watch the rest of it and make sure there's nothing embarrassing on it — "

"Lucy?"

"I know, I'm babbling." Lucy stopped and laughed. "Sorry. I was really scared for a while. I guess I'm still a little nervous."

Robert looked at her, and Lucy saw the same look she'd seen on Jenny's face — skepticism.

"Listen," she said, not wanting to make a fool of herself by begging him to stay. "I'm okay, now. Thanks for the notes."

But maybe he wasn't as skeptical as she

thought, because he said, "Tell you what, Lucy. Give me a flashlight and I'll take a look around outside for you, okay?"

At least he'd offered, Lucy thought, feeling relieved. Thanking him again, she went into the kitchen, found the flashlight, and brought it to him. Then she waited by the front door and listened as he walked around the outside of the house. She could hear him crunching in the leaves and grass, but the sound didn't frighten her this time. She was almost sorry when it stopped.

"All clear," Robert reported, trotting up the steps onto the porch and handing her the flashlight. "Not that I really knew what I was looking for, but nobody's lurking in the bushes, that much I could tell."

Nobody's lurking, Lucy thought as she watched Robert head back down the steps. Not now.

But someone had been.

And they might be back.

Snow had fallen during the night, and it was still snowing lightly when Lucy went to school the next morning. Too bad it hadn't happened sooner, she thought. Then Robert would have found footprints outside the house.

But if he had, what would she have done? The police wouldn't come running because someone had walked around outside her house. What did she have to do? Wait until something happened to her? Not to her locker or her book bag, but to *her*?

"Stalkers don't usually do that, do they?" she asked as Jenny joined her in the hallway.

"Hi to you, too." Jenny pushed back the hood of the rain poncho she'd borrowed from Lucy. "What are you talking about? What don't stalkers usually do?"

"Hurt people."

"I don't know. You're the expert," Jenny said.

Lucy frowned at her. "It's not funny, you know. And it's not my imagination. I didn't *imagine* that somebody was outside my house last night, before anyone else came home. I almost called the police."

Jenny's eyes widened. "What happened? Why didn't you?"

Lucy told her how Robert had come and then looked around. "He didn't see anybody, naturally. Someone was there, though. But if I called the police now, they'd never believe it. Or they wouldn't be able to do anything." They'd reached her locker and she pulled out the slip of paper with the new combination on it. She opened the locker and peered inside. Good, everything was the same as she'd left it.

"Anyway," she went on, stuffing a couple of books on the shelf, "I was trying to convince myself that I really don't have that much to worry about because if the stalker *hurts* the stalkee, then the fun's over, right?"

"Like I said, I don't know." Jenny held up her hand, as if she thought Lucy was going to snap at her. "I'm not making fun, really. I just don't know."

"But you still think I'm imagining things, don't you?"

"I never said that." Jenny looked insulted. "I guess I just think it sounds too weird to be true, that's all."

"Yeah, I know what you mean." Lucy smiled. "Sorry. It's just spooky. Oh," she added, "I brought Allen's tape." She patted her duffel bag. "Maybe we could meet in the lab after school and you can show me how to erase the part I want to get rid of."

"Sure." Jenny turned to go, then turned back. "Listen, try not to worry, okay? I know it's spooky, but you still don't know for sure that someone's after you. Maybe we can come up with a way to find out."

"What if we do?" Lucy asked. "Find out if it's true, I mean."

Jenny grinned. "*Then* you can worry."

Lucy felt better after that, just knowing that Jenny was on her side. They'd been friends since seventh grade and never had a major fight. Jenny was smart, and she noticed things; if anybody could help Lucy figure this out, she could. She was fearless, too. If there was a stalker, she'd probably sit on him while Lucy called the police.

But what if there wasn't? What if it was all too weird to be true, like Jenny said? By lunch, when Robert couldn't resist telling everybody how he'd crept around her house with a flashlight, looking behind bushes and hoping none of the neighbors would see him, Lucy was even able to laugh about it.

"I couldn't help it," she said. "I guess I overreacted, but I was really scared."

"I don't see why you're laughing," Suzanne said. "I read about this television actress who was stalked, and the stalker killed her."

"Thanks a lot, Suzanne," Lucy said.

"Yeah, Suze," Robert said. "We're trying to cheer Lucy up, not make her paranoid."

"All I'm saying is she should be careful," Suzanne said. She looked at Lucy and her blue eyes, usually cool and distant, were bright and almost piercing. "It might not be a joke."

Lucy shifted in her chair and looked at Jon, who was sitting at the end of the table. He was watching her, a small smile playing around his mouth. He kept quiet, but he seemed to be telling her not to pay any attention to Suzanne.

Lucy glanced back at Suzanne. "Thanks, Suzanne," she said. "I promise I'll be careful. Anyway, if I *am* getting paranoid, I'm pretty sure I know why. It's because I have a ghost."

Robert put his head in his hands, as if he couldn't believe he was hearing this.

"Seriously," Lucy said. "It's Allen. Sometimes I dream that I can hear him playing basketball next door. Yesterday, before Robert came over, I fell asleep, and I heard his voice. Allen's voice, I mean."

Lucy stopped. Everyone was staring at her now. Even Brad, who usually stared at Suzanne, had his eyes on her.

She laughed. "It's not what you think," she told them. "I don't really believe there's a ghost. What I mean is, I still think about him a lot."

"You're not the only one," Suzanne said. Her voice was high and tight.

"I know." Lucy sighed. "Oh, never mind, I can't say it right. But anyway, you know that video I have? The one his mother gave me? I'm going to edit it. Well, Jenny's going to do it and I'm going to help. We're starting after school today, and when we're done, we'll have a kind of movie."

"Sounds nice," Brad said. "But Allen won't be in it."

"Well, I haven't seen it all yet," Lucy said. "Maybe he got somebody to take shots of him. But that's not the point."

"What is?" Suzanne asked.

"It'll be something special from Allen," Lucy said. "A movie of us. His friends."

Chapter 10

At the end of the day, Lucy stopped at her locker and got the stuff she'd need for homework, then made her way through the halls to the video lab.

Busy this time. At least ten kids were in the room, moving back and forth between monitors and recorders, calling out numbers that made no sense to Lucy, arguing with each other and all talking at the tops of their voices.

Jenny was in the middle of it all, but she didn't look upset. She looked as if she was loving every minute of it. Robert was there, too, but he had a pained expression on his face. Robert obviously didn't like chaos.

"Hi," Lucy said to Jenny, after she'd picked her way through the crowd. "I guess this isn't the best time for us to work."

"It'll clear out soon," Jenny said. "I think. Give it about fifteen minutes."

Lucy found an empty chair and dragged it against one of the walls, so she'd be out of the way. Robert left, still looking pained, and that reminded her — she hadn't even started to study for the history test yet. She took the notes out of her bag and looked them over.

A couple of minutes later, she got up and went over to Jenny. "Listen," she said, "I think I'd better go."

"Why? In ten more minutes, half these guys'll be gone," Jenny said, logging numbers into a notebook. "I'll still be here, of course. I have the feeling I'm going to be here forever."

"I just looked at the stuff I have to know for a test," Lucy explained. "If I don't get started now, it'll be a disaster. Plus I have a ton of other work, too."

"Well, okay. Oh, I know," Jenny said. "Give me the tape, why don't you? I have to make a copy and I can do it now. Or sometime before I leave, anyway. It'll save us time."

"Good idea." Lucy gave her the tape and said good-bye. Jenny waved, her head already bent over her work again.

The snow, unusual for November, had turned to rain. From her seat on the bus, Lucy could look down and see the slush splashing up from behind the giant tires as the bus lurched away from the stop across the street from school. She'd missed the school bus, but she'd checked the town bus schedule last night, knowing she'd be leaving late anyway. The town bus would let her off half a block from her house.

What could go wrong on a one-minute walk?

Maybe a lot.

But maybe nothing. Especially if you watch out, Lucy told herself.

Settling back for the short ride, she gazed out the window. Saw Suzanne standing at the corner, talking to Dave Travis, not Brad. Brad was on the wrestling team; maybe that's where he was now.

The bus stopped to let passengers on and off. A car whizzed by and Lucy turned her head to watch. The driver looked like Jon, but the car was past before she could tell. Couldn't have been him, anyway. He didn't have the car very often.

Facing front again, Lucy thought about Jon. Not about the look on his face in Allen's video, or when she told him about her locker. She thought about his gray eyes and dark-blond hair, and the way he'd smiled at lunch. And she wished he'd ask her out again.

He'd said he would, but he hadn't. Of course, they'd gone out Saturday and this was only Tuesday. She should wait.

But she didn't want to. So what was stopping *her* from making a date? Nothing.

The bus reached Lucy's stop and she got out. She'd been planning to hurry the half-block to her house. Actually, she'd been planning to run. Instead, she walked steadily and only looked behind her twice.

When she let herself in, the cat went out, as usual.

When she checked the answering machine, there was a message from her mother, as usual. No other calls.

Even while she went through the house, making sure the doors were locked and nothing was disturbed, Lucy felt her spirits lift.

Everything seemed . . . normal.

Something had been going on, but maybe it was over now. She'd made up that stuff about Allen's ghost today at lunch, but who knew? That might have been what was bothering her, making everything seem different and strange. Making coincidences seem like a plot. Spooking her. Not a real ghost, of course. But a memory.

She couldn't forget Allen. She didn't want to. But she could find a way to get over his death.

One way was to call Jon and make a date herself. Why not? All he could say was no. And she didn't think he would.

There were four Edens in the phone book. She got him on the second try. Well, not him. His brother.

"He's not here," a boy's voice said when Lucy asked for Jon. "Who's this?"

He sounded so suspicious, Lucy thought. "Um, this is Lucy Monroe," she said.

"Yeah?"

"Yes," she said. "Could you tell him I called?"

"Okay."

"And maybe he . . ." Lucy was going to ask for Jon to call back, but his brother had already hung up. What was his name? Brian. Not too friendly. He didn't sound like the kind of kid who'd be interested in a collection of baseball cards.

Not trusting Brian to give Jon her message, Lucy ate an apple, took a shower, and called again. This time there was no answer. She called Jenny. No answer there, either. Jenny was probably still at school.

Okay. No more excuses. It was time to study.

Lucy studied hard the rest of the evening. But whenever the phone rang, she'd lift her head and wait, hoping her mother would say it was for her. Hoping it was Jon.

But Jon didn't call.

Lucy blamed his bratty little brother.

It rained all night, but the sun came out the next morning, for what seemed like the first time in weeks. Lucy decided it was a sign. She was through imagining that a stalker was after her. Never mind what Suzanne said about that actress, never mind what Lucy herself had been thinking.

The things that happened — the calls and the footsteps and her locker — had really happened. She hadn't imagined them. But they weren't connected. *She* was the one who'd connected them; now it was time to break them apart.

Jenny would be glad to hear it, Lucy thought, running up the school steps. Jenny had been trying to tell her the same thing all along.

Jenny wasn't in the hallway, but Jon was. Just ahead of her, walking fast like he usually did.

Smiling when she realized it was him, Lucy scurried up behind him and tapped him on the shoulder. "I have a complaint," she said.

At the sound of her voice, Jon whirled around. His face changed from a sleepy-eyed look to one of complete surprise.

"Hey," Lucy laughed. "It's just me."

For a second, she thought he looked angry. But the expression was gone so fast she decided she must have imagined it. Why would he be angry at her, anyway?

"I guess you didn't get my message," she said as they started walking together.

"Message?" Jon said. "You mean you called?"

Lucy nodded. "Last night. Afternoon, actually."

"I had to work," he said. "It wasn't my day, but somebody was sick so they called me to come in. I didn't want to turn down the pay."

"Well, anyway, I left a message with your brother."

Jon looked at her. "Brian?"

"Well, sure. I mean, I talked to some boy and he didn't say I had the wrong number."

Lucy laughed. "Do you have another brother?"

Jon shook his head, but he didn't laugh with her. "What did you call for?" he asked.

Lucy hesitated. Just because she was in a good mood didn't mean everyone else would be, too. And Jon was not in a good mood. Maybe she should save this for another time.

While she was hesitating, the warning bell rang. She took it as a cue. "It can wait," she said, breaking away to go to her homeroom. "I'll probably see you at lunch and I'll talk to you then."

But by lunch, Lucy had something else on her mind. Something much more important than asking Jon Eden for a date.

At first, when her mood started to slide during homeroom, Lucy blamed it on Jon. Here she'd come to school all happy, ready to make a date with him, ready to start something. And he'd been in a lousy mood. She knew it wasn't his fault, but she still felt disappointed.

She usually passed Jenny in the hall between first and second periods, but today she didn't see her. That was annoying, too. She wanted to tell her how she'd banished the stalker from her mind. How she'd decided not to wait for

Jon to ask her out but to ask him first, and how his bad mood had stopped her. Jenny would tell her to lighten up and try again. Then there was her history exam, which was harder than she'd expected.

But as the morning passed, Lucy realized her spirits weren't sinking because of Jon's mood, or Jenny not being there, or the test.

It was something else, something she couldn't quite put her finger on.

It was like the weather. Waking up and realizing that something was different. Lying in bed and listening. Every sound was muffled. And then you knew: It had snowed during the night.

Or the way the air changed sometimes. When everything got still and the birds got quiet, and even though it was still sunny, you knew a storm was coming.

That's what Lucy was waiting for, she realized. A storm. Not a weather-storm — some other kind. She didn't know what it was, but she could feel it.

Nobody else seemed to feel it. Suzanne looked mad about something. Robert, when Lucy saw him, was whistling, hurrying to his next class. Brad, walking alone, looked a little sad. But nobody looked as if they felt what Lucy felt.

All through the morning, the feeling built. Lucy tried to shake it off, but it wouldn't leave. She tried to tell herself she was imagining it, but she knew she wasn't.

Something was coming. Some kind of storm.

The storm broke just before lunch. Lucy had stopped at her locker and was just heading for the cafeteria when she heard someone say something about Jenny.

Of course, there were five Jennys in the senior class, and probably a dozen more in the school, but Lucy stopped anyway.

Two friends of Robert's were standing by the water fountain. Vicki and Diane. Looking excited, shocked. The same look some of the kids had had when they found out about Allen.

Lucy moved closer.

"She shouldn't have been walking home alone after dark, I guess," Vicki was saying now. "I mean, this is supposed to be a safe town, but you never know."

Diane nodded in agreement, her eyes wide. "When did you find out?" she asked breathlessly.

"Just a few minutes ago," Vicki said. "I was

in the office when her mother called. Everybody got all upset. It was crazy."

Lucy hadn't heard the name Jenny again, but she had to make sure. "Excuse me," she said. "Who are you guys talking about?"

The two girls turned their heads and saw Lucy. Then they exchanged quick glances.

Lucy felt the storm building, getting much closer.

"I heard you say 'Jenny,'" she said. "You're not talking about Jenny Berger, are you?"

Diane slid her eyes back to Vicki, waiting for her to take the lead.

Vicki took a deep breath.

"You *are* talking about Jenny Berger," Lucy said. It wasn't a question. The storm was right over her head now.

Both girls nodded, their heads bobbing up and down in time together. Then Vicki said, "Oh, Lucy, I feel just awful. Jenny's your best friend, isn't she?"

Chapter 11

Lucy felt her lips go numb. She wanted to ask questions, but her mouth wouldn't work. Vicki's and Diane's faces hung in front of her like pale moons, their expressions avid with curiosity. Was Lucy going to scream or cry or something exciting like that?

Lucy tried to think. "Jenny's your best friend," Vicki had said. Jenny *is*. That was important.

"She's not dead," Lucy said.

Vicki's mouth snapped shut, then opened again. "No, she's not dead!" she gasped. "I never said she was dead. But she was hurt. What I heard was . . ."

The words came spilling out, but Lucy didn't wait around to hear them. Not from Vicki, who'd probably get it all wrong.

Lucy hurried through the halls to the office,

hoping they wouldn't tell her to get to class and keep calm. School people got that way sometimes. Secretive and hush-hush. As if teenagers were emotional weaklings who'd fall apart at bad news.

The locker lady was in the office again.

Lucy wished it were Suzanne. At least Suzanne would answer her questions. The locker lady patted her hair and looked flustered. "Honey, she's all right," she said to Lucy. "She's in the hospital, but she's going to be fine. Now then," she said, glancing at the clock. "Isn't it your lunchtime?"

"But I just want to know what happened," Lucy said. "She's my best friend. What's the big deal?"

The locker lady looked at Lucy and her eyes softened. "Honey, I don't know the details. I hardly know the main story. If I did, I'd tell you."

Lucy sighed and managed a small smile. "Okay. Thanks."

She left the office and started toward the cafeteria. Halfway there, she stopped and turned around. She went to her locker, got her jacket, then went down another hall and left the building through a side door.

She'd decided to skip lunch. Food could wait. So could school.

"The" hospital. Bridgetown had two of them. Lucy had run across the street to catch a bus, but then she realized she had no idea which hospital to go to. She didn't want to waste a lot of time going to the wrong one first.

She could go back and ask the locker lady, but now that she was out of the school, she didn't want to go inside again. If only she had her own car.

A bus was lumbering down the street, and Lucy made up her mind: She'd go home and call the hospitals. Once she knew where Jenny was, she'd call and then decide what to do.

The house was quiet when Lucy let herself in. A couple of days ago, she would have checked every door, looked in closets, and listened for clicks on the answering machine.

Not this time. Lucy kicked off her shoes and headed for the kitchen, not thinking about herself for once. Thinking about her best friend.

Searching for the phone book, Lucy kept wondering what had happened. Vicki had said something about walking alone at night and how it wasn't safe. Did Jenny get hit by a car? Robbed at gunpoint? Did people really get robbed at gunpoint in boring old Bridgetown? Why hadn't Lucy let Vicki tell her what she knew? Maybe Vicki knew more than the locker lady.

There was the phone book — on top of the refrigerator. Lucy pulled it off and sat at the table, looking for the hospital numbers. Moe meandered in, blinking sleepily. Then he leapt onto the table and purred at her while she looked up the numbers.

Jenny was at Bridgetown General, room 454. Lucy asked to be connected, but when nobody answered after five rings, she hung up.

The cat curled up on the open phone book while Lucy chewed on a fingernail, thinking. It was a good sign that they rang Jenny's room, wasn't it? They wouldn't do that if she was in terrible shape, would they? (Of course she wasn't in terrible shape — didn't the locker lady say she'd be fine?)

Jenny was in the bathroom, or being X-rayed or something, that was all. Or maybe she was checking out.

Lucy picked up the phone again and called

Jenny's home. No answer. No answering machine, either, so she couldn't leave a message.

Frustrated, Lucy chewed another fingernail and tried to decide. She could stay here and keep calling the hospital. Or she could just catch a bus and go there.

Sitting around waiting would be worse. Leaving Moe curled on the telephone book, Lucy put her shoes back on, left the house, and headed for the hospital.

As Lucy walked the half-block to catch her bus, her mind was on Jenny, not on hang-up phone calls, or footsteps in the yard at night. If she'd been thinking about them, she might have looked back. If she'd looked back, she might have noticed the car that rolled slowly down the street and coasted to a stop near Allen's house. If she'd noticed it, she might have recognized it.

But Lucy's mind was on Jenny, and she didn't look back.

When Lucy got to room 454 at the hospital, Mrs. Berger was just coming out the door. She looked tired, and maybe a little worried, but that was all. No tears. Lucy had already been told that Jenny was okay, and when she saw Mrs. Berger's face, she really believed it.

"Lucy, what are you . . . ?" Mrs. Berger stopped and shook her head. "Never mind, I know what you're doing here. If it had been you, Jenny would have cut school, too. She'd be thrilled to see you, but she's asleep right now."

Jenny's mother pushed open the door, and Lucy peeked inside. There was Jenny, a bandage on one side of her face and a cast on her left arm. Her face was pale.

Lucy waited until she saw for sure that Jenny was breathing, then she pulled back into the hall.

"What happened?" she asked.

Jenny's mother sighed. "Come on with me to the coffee shop," she said. "If I don't have something with caffeine in it, I'll fall asleep standing up."

Over coffee and cocoa, Jenny's mother told Lucy what she knew. Jenny had stayed late at the video lab, putting a music track onto a ten-minute tape for some project that was due in a few days.

"She called home at six," Mrs. Berger said.

"Told me she'd be another hour, at least. Well, I said I'd come get her, but she said no, somebody was always around the lab, she'd catch a ride. And if she didn't, she'd call me again."

Lucy sipped some cocoa, then warmed her hands on the Styrofoam cup. "But she didn't call?"

"Oh, she called," Mrs. Berger said. "But she said there wasn't any answer. I must have been in the basement and didn't hear the phone." She thought a moment. "Or maybe it was when I went out to get the mail — it was late yesterday." She sighed again. "Anyway, Jenny was ready to leave and she got impatient. And of course, we're only a twenty-minute walk away."

Lucy waited.

"She left the school alone. I guess everyone else had gone by then," Mrs. Berger said. "And — she was a little fuzzy about the details — but about two blocks from the school, she said she heard someone walking behind her."

Stalking her, Lucy thought with a shiver.

"Well, she didn't even glance around. Not that it would have done any good," Mrs. Berger went on. "Before she knew what was happening, somebody had grabbed her from behind. This is where it gets fuzzy," she added, "but Jenny tried to fight."

Lucy almost smiled. Naturally, Jenny would fight.

"There was one hell of a struggle, and somehow Jenny's wrist got broken, and her head bashed against the concrete," Mrs. Berger said. "But then the attacker ran off, thank God. After he snatched her bag with all her money in it, of course."

"Did she see him?" Lucy asked.

Mrs. Berger shook her head. "It was dark by then, and they were on a side street, and somehow he always managed to stay behind her. No cars came by — isn't that always the way?" She drank some more coffee. "I shouldn't be bitter. I should be grateful that it wasn't worse."

Lucy nodded. "How did you find out?"

"Jenny said that while it was happening, she was too busy struggling to even open her mouth. Then she was unconscious for a little while. When she came to, she screamed bloody murder!" Mrs. Berger almost laughed. "Someone in one of the houses heard her and called the police."

Lucy's cocoa was cold by now, but she finished it anyway. "Thank God she's all right."

"Yes." Jenny's mother looked at the clock on the wall of the coffee shop. "I should go back now," she said. "Jenny can probably come home tomorrow — they just want to 'observe' her for the rest of the night because of concussion. But I'm keeping her home the rest of the week."

"Tell her I was here, okay?" Lucy said. "And I'll come see her tomorrow."

"After school," Mrs. Berger said. "Don't you go cutting school again, Lucy. She's going to be fine."

Lucy smiled. "I'll bet she'll try to make some kind of film out of it," she said. "She won't talk about how scared she was, she'll talk about how dramatic it was. She'll probably try to re-stage it and get it on tape."

Mrs. Berger laughed. Then she said, "Oh, I almost forgot. Jenny was babbling a lot last night, but one thing she was clear about: She said, 'Tell Lucy her tape's okay.'"

Lucy didn't get it for a second. Then she remembered — Jenny was going to make a copy of Allen's tape for her.

"She had a videotape in her bag," Mrs. Berger went on, "but it wasn't yours. It was hers. She kept saying that yours was all right, it was in the lab, along with a copy." Mrs. Berger laughed again. "Of course, your raincoat's a total loss, I'm afraid."

"What? Oh," Lucy said, remembering the yellow poncho Jenny had borrowed. "That doesn't matter. When she wakes up, remind her that I didn't like it anyway."

Relief made Lucy tired, and when she got off the bus, the half-block home seemed like half a mile. At least Jenny was all right, she thought, trudging up the front walk. At least she hadn't been raped, or killed. The attacker had only been after money.

With one hand on the front doorknob, Lucy fumbled for her key, found it, and stuck it in the lock.

The door opened easily. Differently. It felt like it didn't need the key. Had she been in such a hurry that she'd gone and left it unlocked?

Lucy had been tired from relief, but now she tensed up again. Was it her imagination, or had the door really been unlocked when she'd opened it?

Nervously, Lucy moved down the hall, peering into the den and living room. Nothing seemed disturbed. The kitchen looked the same, too, except the cat wasn't on the phone book any longer.

Down the hall to the bedrooms. Everything looked normal. There was a dent in her pillow where the cat had slept, and that was normal, too. It was one of his favorite places.

Out in the hall again, Lucy stood still and listened. She heard the refrigerator, her clock, the furnace. Regular noises.

She must have imagined the door.

Tiredness hit her again, and Lucy yawned so hard her eyes teared. It was only three-thirty, but she felt as if she'd been awake for days without sleep.

In her bedroom, Lucy took off her shoes and stretched out on the bed. She'd sleep for half an hour or so, then call Jenny at the hospital.

Just as she was drifting off, Lucy heard the noise.

She rolled to her side and tried to ignore it. It was only Moe at the back door, scratching to get in. He'd give up in a minute.

But the cat didn't give up. If Lucy didn't let him in, he'd keep scratching and she'd never get to sleep.

Yawning again, Lucy rolled off the bed, went to the kitchen, and pulled open the back door.

The cat came in and rubbed against her legs and then stared up at her: Time for a snack.

Lucy was reaching for the box of cat treats on the counter when her hand stopped in mid-air. Her heart started to pound, and she felt that prickling sensation on the back of her neck.

The cat had been in the kitchen when she left. Snoozing on the phone book, right there on the table.

How had he gotten out of the house?

Chapter 12

"He slipped out when you did," Lucy's mother said later when they were eating dinner. "You just didn't see him."

Lucy took a bite of salad and thought back to when she'd run out of the house. She'd left Moe sleeping on the table, at least she thought she had. But he was a cat, after all, and cats had a way of moving around like shadows. Half the time she wouldn't realize he'd left one room until she saw him in another.

"I guess maybe he did," Lucy said doubtfully. "But what about the door?"

"I don't know, maybe you did leave it unlocked," Mrs. Monroe said, getting up for some coffee. "But that doesn't mean someone came inside. Nothing's missing or disturbed, you said."

Lucy shook her head. "I looked all over

again after I let Moe in. If anything's gone, I can't tell."

Her mother laughed. "Well, if anyone came in and took something and we haven't missed it by now, we'll probably never miss it." She sat back down at the table and stirred some sugar into her coffee. "I think your imagination's working overtime. You're jittery because of Jenny," she said.

"Well, you're right about Jenny." Lucy got up to fix a plate of food for her father, who'd called saying he'd be late. "It must have been really scary," she said, spooning rice onto the plate. "I still can't believe it."

Lucy had called the hospital again and finally talked to Jenny. She was tired and sore, but already griping about the food. "It's worse than what we get at school," she'd said. "Mom's out getting me some pizza right now."

Lucy smiled. "I don't suppose you want to tell me all the gory details," she said.

"Are you kidding? It wouldn't be any fun if I couldn't do that!"

Jenny didn't have many more details than her mother had already told Lucy, but she described everything much more dramatically. "Imagine it," she'd said. "You're walking along the dark street. Alone. You hear footsteps on the pavement behind you. They're slow at first, but then they get faster."

Lucy shuddered. She could imagine it very well. "I guess it's good that you can joke about it," she said. "You could have been killed."

"Yeah, well . . ." Jenny's voice trailed off. Then she said, "Hey, but I hurt him, too, you know."

"You did? How?"

"I used my fingernails," Jenny said. "First I kept trying to turn around so I could push better. But he had one arm around me from behind and he was pulling my hood over my face with his other hand. Well, *your* hood, I should say."

"What? Oh, right, my poncho," Lucy said.

"Right. So I tried to scratch his face, but I had to settle for his arm. His sleeve got all pulled up and I managed to rake him really hard."

Lucy shuddered again. Too bad it wasn't his face, she thought. He couldn't hide that. But his arm? It was long-sleeve weather. He was safe.

"Did he get much money?" she asked.

"When did I ever have much money?" Jenny

snorted. "Anyway, it's my tape I'm mad about. I have a backup, thank God, but I still have to lay the music track down again."

The two of them had talked a few minutes longer. Then Jenny got really sleepy and they'd hung up.

Now, putting plastic wrap over the plate of food, Lucy thought about the conversation some more. Something kept poking at the back of her mind. Was it something Jenny had said? Or not said? Maybe it didn't have anything to do with the conversation at all. Maybe it was something else.

Or maybe she was still just jittery, Lucy thought.

But she couldn't get rid of the feeling.

Lucy didn't notice anyone standing by her locker the next morning until she heard the rapping. Still bothered by the feeling of the night before, she jumped and hit her elbow hard on the metal edge of the door.

"Sorry," Jon said. The smiling Jon this time. "Didn't mean to scare you."

"It's okay." Lucy rubbed her elbow, then finished putting her stuff away. "I'm edgy, as my mom says." She shut the locker. "I guess you heard about Jenny."

He nodded, his smile fading. "Everybody was talking about it yesterday. I thought I'd see you at lunch, but after I heard what happened, I figured you'd gone to the hospital. Did you see her?"

"She was asleep," Lucy said. "But I talked to her later. She's okay. She's going home today."

"So what did she say?" Jon asked as they walked down the hall. "I mean, did she see the guy or what?"

Lucy shook her head. "She said she scratched him, though. Too bad she only got his arm and not his eyes." She looked at Jon. "I'll bet when you moved here, everybody told you it was a nice, quiet town."

"You're right, they did," he said, laughing a little. "But stuff like this happens everywhere, I guess."

"It must have been drugs," Lucy said. "Somebody was probably after money for drugs." She laughed, too. "Jenny didn't have much with her, so I'm glad the guy was disappointed. All he got, really, was her videotape, and he can't do anything with that."

"Yeah, listen, Lucy," Jon said quickly. "You want to go out again? Saturday, maybe?"

Lucy blinked, a little startled at the quick

change of subject. And Jon looked uncomfortable, almost shy. He hadn't been shy when he'd asked her out the first time. So why now?

Who cares? she told herself. It's what you were going to ask him yesterday, so just be glad and say yes.

"Yes," she said.

Making the date with Jon helped Lucy's mood, but she still couldn't shake that funny feeling. Like she'd forgotten something, or lost something. But she didn't even know what she was looking for. She just missed it.

At lunch, since she was Jenny's best friend and knew more than anyone, Lucy found herself telling an entire table of kids about the mugging.

Jon was there, and Suzanne and Brad. Dave Travis sat next to Robert. Vicki and Diane pulled their chairs over so they could get the facts straight.

Lucy wasn't exactly getting tired of talking about it, but she *had* been telling bits and pieces of the story all morning. Maybe that's why her mind wandered, even while she was talking.

And maybe that's why she finally put her finger on what had been bothering her.

She was in the middle of telling them what Jenny had said about the struggle. "She was trying to turn around so she could push him," Lucy said, "but he — "

"All she needed to do was stomp down real hard on his foot," Vicki said. "I read that someplace. You stomp on somebody's foot the right way and it mashes their arch. Or something like that."

"No, what she needed to do was kick him — you know where," Diane said.

"According to Lucy, she couldn't do that," Suzanne said. "Right, Lucy? Jenny couldn't turn around so she couldn't see him. Or kick him," she added.

Lucy was hardly listening. Whatever she'd forgotten, or lost, was just outside her mind's eye. What was it?

"Sorry," Vicki said. "Go ahead, Lucy."

Lucy dragged her mind back to the conversation. "Right, she couldn't turn around," she said slowly. "He was holding too tight and he was pulling her hood over her face."

Lucy stopped. It was closer now. What was it?

She shook her head. "Where was I?" she asked.

"The hood," Vicki said. "He was pulling her

hood over her face." She turned to the others. "That's so she wouldn't see who he was," she explained. "So she couldn't identify him later."

Lucy stared at her. "What did you say?"

Vicki blushed slightly and shifted around in her chair. "Okay, so I watch too much television," she said. "But that's the way it always goes — the attacker tries to make sure the victim can't identify him. That's why this creep pulled the hood over Jenny's face."

Lucy kept staring. But she wasn't really seeing Vicki.

Instead, she was seeing Jenny. Walking alone on a dark, rainy street. Her duffel bag — the same blue canvas as Lucy's — slung over one shoulder. Her hair — almost the same color as Lucy's — spilling out from underneath the hood of a poncho.

A neon-yellow poncho.

Lucy's poncho.

"Well? Aren't you going to finish?" Vicki asked.

Lucy's eyes focused on the present again. Vicki's face hung there, avid for details, just like yesterday. Diane was leaning forward expectantly.

The others were watching her, too. Jon's

eyes were narrowed. Robert was frowning at her. Suzanne held her spoon above a cup of yogurt and sat very still, waiting for Lucy to finish.

Lucy swallowed. "So she scratched his arm," she said. "And he pushed and she fell and hit her head. You probably know the rest." She swallowed again, then scraped her chair back and stood up quickly. She had to get out of there so she could think. "Listen, I just remembered something I have to do," she told them. "I'll see you later, or . . ."

Leaving her sentence unfinished, Lucy turned away and hurried out of the cafeteria.

Ducking into the first bathroom she came to, Lucy shut herself into a stall and waited. She heard the bell ring and footsteps thunder down the hall. The bathroom door opened and closed a hundred times while she waited and listened to girls talking about boys and teachers and movies and homework.

The bell rang again, and the bathroom emptied. After a moment, Lucy opened the stall door and came out.

At the sink, she ran the cold water and splashed her face. Drying it on a rough paper towel, she glanced in the mirror.

A little pale, but the same Lucy Monroe. Long brown hair, blue eyes, nothing out of the ordinary about her.

Unless she put on a bright yellow poncho. Then she'd stand out, even at night on a dark, rainy street.

Which is exactly what Jenny had done.

Whoever had attacked Jenny had meant to attack *Lucy*.

Gripping the edges of the sink, Lucy leaned closer to the mirror. He meant to get *you*, she thought, looking at her reflection.

She hadn't imagined the stalker after all. He was real. He'd gone through her locker and her bag. He'd called her home. He'd probably even been in her house yesterday.

But he wasn't just stalking. She'd been wrong about that. He was after something.

And suddenly Lucy knew what it was.

Turning from the mirror, Lucy looked down at her fraying canvas duffel bag.

Jenny had been carrying one like it. That's what the attacker was after. Something in the bag.

What had Jenny been so mad about losing? Not her money or her notebooks. Her videotape.

But the attacker hadn't been after Jenny's tape. He'd thought he was attacking Lucy.

He was after Allen's videotape.

Lucy picked up her bag and slung it over her shoulder. No time to waste, she thought, spinning around and hurrying out of the bathroom. The attacker knew he'd gotten the wrong one, that's why he'd come into her house yesterday. In a rush, worrying about Jenny, Lucy must have left the door unlocked. And whoever was after the tape had walked right in. He hadn't found it, of course. It wasn't in her house, and it wasn't in her duffel bag.

It was in the video lab, and Lucy had to get it.

Because there was something on that tape. And whatever it was, someone was desperate to keep it a secret.

Chapter 13

The tape was in the video lab, just as Jenny had said. Lucy found it in the big walk-in closet with the thick metal door where tapes were kept to protect them from fire and water and whatever else could damage them. It wasn't labeled, but Lucy recognized it from the Z-shaped scratch on its plastic casing.

If whoever wanted it had come looking for it, they hadn't found it. Lucy had it now.

There were a couple of kids in the lab when Lucy went in, but neither one of them had paid any attention to her. With the tape safe at the bottom of her bag, she left the lab and went on to her next class.

No one who mattered had seen her.

But who mattered?

Suzanne, Brad, Robert, and Jon. There were other kids on the tape, but only those four knew that Allen's mother had given it to

Lucy. Only those four had heard Lucy say she was going to work on it in the lab. They were the four who mattered. Suzanne, Brad, Robert, and Jon.

All of them? One of them?

Paying almost no attention to anything that went on in her classes, Lucy played the tape back in her mind.

Kids at the car wash. Robert directing the traffic. People walking on the street. Suzanne and Brad dancing at Allen's on the Fourth of July.

Jon at Robert's party, looking angry.

Every time Lucy remembered that part of the tape, she felt like crying. Then she felt like yelling. Had she been fooling herself about him? She knew he'd changed. He'd always been so cool and aloof, until after she gave him the basketball and talked about the tape. Then he'd suddenly become friendly. He'd acted interested in her. He'd asked her out. Was it just because he wanted the tape?

But why would he want it so badly? It showed him getting angry at Allen for something, that was all. You didn't go through someone's locker or sneak into someone's house because of that. You didn't mug someone.

But she hadn't seen all of the tape. The VCR

had broken right after that scene. There could be more on it that Jon didn't want anyone to look at.

Or there could be more on it that someone else didn't want her to see. But it was one of those four.

Lucy knew she'd have to watch the rest of the tape, but no one had taken the VCR in for repairs yet. When school was over, she called Jenny, asking if she could come over and watch it at her house. Jenny was home, but she was busy packing.

"Packing?" Lucy asked. "What for? I thought you were going to take it easy for a few days."

"I am," Jenny said. "I'm just going to take it easy at my grandparents'. We were going to go up Friday for their anniversary anyway, and stay the weekend. But since I'm home, Mom decided we'll just go up a day early."

"How are you feeling?" Lucy asked.

"Okay. I feel fine, actually," Jenny said. "Listen, I've got to leave in about fifteen minutes. I'm glad you called — I'll see you on Monday, okay?"

Lucy said good-bye and hung up. She hadn't had a chance to ask about using Jenny's VCR, but it didn't matter. Nobody would be there.

But Lucy couldn't wait for Jenny to come back. She couldn't wait for their VCR to be fixed. She had to see the tape.

The phone Lucy had used was near the gym. Basketball practice was going on; she could hear the running and thumping and yelling. It reminded her of Allen. And Jon.

Keeping a tight hold on the strap of her duffel bag, Lucy walked down the hall and turned the corner. Now she was near the video lab.

Why not? she thought. The lab had plenty of VCRs and monitors. She could go in there and watch her tape. Nobody would ask any questions, not if she acted as if she belonged there.

The only one of the four she had to watch out for in the lab was Robert. But Lucy happened to know that Student Council was meeting right now. And Robert, naturally, was president.

How could Robert be the one? He was her friend. But they all were.

This whole thing was hard to believe. As Lucy walked into the video lab, she had to remind herself that it was really happening.

Three kids were in the lab, all of them hunched over equipment, editing tapes. None of them looked at her.

Acting as if she used this place all the time, Lucy walked to a table on the far side of the room where one of the recorders and monitors was set up. To get there, she had to go behind some tall metal shelves stacked with cables and empty tape boxes and equipment that was broken or not being used. She couldn't see the door from here. But if anyone came in, anyone who mattered, they wouldn't see her, either.

Taking Allen's tape out of her bag, Lucy turned on the recorder and slipped the tape into the slot.

"You're not going to see much," a voice said.

Startled, Lucy looked around. It was a guy who'd been busy editing. Now he was watching her.

"What's the matter?" he asked. "You jumped about a foot."

"Yeah, well . . ." Lucy said, "nothing's the matter." She smiled at him, trying to look calm and relaxed. "Why aren't I going to see much?"

He pointed. "Monitor's not on."

Lucy looked at the blank screen. "Right."

She turned the monitor on, pulled a chair over, and sat down.

The tape had already played for a few seconds, so Lucy rewound it. Just as she was about to start it up again, the guy said, "What are you working on?"

His voice was much closer now. He'd left his editing and come over to stand behind her chair.

Lucy took her hand off the play button. "I'm not working, really," she said. "I mean, I am, but it's nothing special. Sort of a home movie." She wished the guy would go back to what he'd been doing.

Instead, he moved closer and leaned against the table. "Term project?" he asked. Then he laughed. "What else could it be, right? They're due next week."

With that, he was off, talking about his own project. Lucy listened with one ear. Video people could talk forever about angles and lighting and cutaways and stuff. Jenny did it all the time, sometimes until Lucy's eyes glazed over with boredom.

She wasn't bored now, though. She was just impatient to see Allen's tape. The guy didn't seem to notice, he just kept chatting. Every time he paused, Lucy would reach out to the recorder as if she were going to get started, but he didn't take the hint.

Finally, though, he ran out of steam. "Well," he said, "I've got to go. Good luck with the project."

"Right, thanks." Lucy thought he'd go back to his work, but instead, he shut off his equipment, picked up some books, and left the room.

Everything was quiet.

Lucy stood up and walked around the metal shelves. The room was empty now. While the guy had been talking, the two other kids must have left.

She was alone now.

She wasn't sure she liked it.

Maybe it was better this way, though. She didn't want anyone to come stand behind her and watch, just out of curiosity. She didn't know what might be on the tape.

Still, the room was awfully quiet.

So was the hallway. Lucy couldn't hear anyone walking by or talking out there. She moved to the open door and looked up and down the hall. Empty, like the lab.

No one knew she was there now. Maybe that was good.

Trying to shake off her nervousness, Lucy went back behind the shelves, sat down, and started the tape.

At first, she thought she'd fast-forward to the spot where her VCR had gone on the blink. But now Lucy decided to start at the beginning of the tape. When she'd watched it before, she hadn't been looking past the surface. Maybe if she watched it closely, she'd notice something. Something that someone didn't want seen.

It started with the car wash. Kids clowning around with the hoses, getting sopping wet, tossing suds at each other. Robert directing cars, waving his arms like a policeman. More clowning around, drops of water on the lens.

To Lucy, everything looked normal.

On to the street scene. Lucy sat forward and peered intently at the screen. Had she missed something in these shots? Was one of the four in here someplace?

People walked by, averting their eyes from the camera. Or making funny faces at it. All of them were strangers to Lucy.

She stopped the tape and rolled it back. This time, she looked at the buildings instead of the faces. She recognized a pizza place, and a stationery store. Allen had been shooting on Poplar Street.

But she couldn't see inside the stores, and Allen had never aimed the camera at the street itself, so she couldn't see any cars or drivers.

If there was a secret hidden there, Lucy couldn't see it.

On to Allen's July Fourth party. Suzanne and Brad dancing, close together. The only thing new Lucy saw was Dave Travis, who was looking very serious. Much too serious for a party. But then the camera moved on, and she didn't see him again.

Another street scene, then the shot of the sky and treetops. Robert's party was next.

Suddenly Lucy stopped the tape.

She thought she heard a noise.

The recorder whirred and clicked. Then there was silence.

Lucy waited, listening. Nothing.

She leaned sideways, bending low, and tried to see through the tall metal shelves that hid her from most of the room. From this position, she could see the bottom half of the doorway.

It was empty.

But someone could already have come in.

Straightening, Lucy got up, scraping the chair back and loudly clearing her throat. No one peered around the shelves to see who was making so much noise.

No one else was here.

But just in case, Lucy took a quick walk around the room. Another glance out the door. Nobody.

She moved the door back and forth. It squeaked a little. She eased it partway closed. If someone came in, at least she'd hear them.

Back at the table, Lucy pressed play and sat down to watch the rest of the tape.

There was Robert's party. The shot of the photograph of Robert standing next to his car. Then on to the people — Jenny, Brad, Suzanne, Dave. Robert wasn't in it — was that important? How could it be? If he wasn't in the shot, then he didn't have anything to hide.

And there was Jon. Standing up, holding out his hand. Turning his back and walking away.

Lucy tensed. The "big" scene was coming up.

She watched it through slitted eyes, not wanting to see Jon's angry face, but not wanting to miss anything.

The scene looked the same as it had before. Mean. Almost scary.

But still, it was only a few seconds on a video. Less than half a minute of Jon, looking and acting mad. It might be something he'd be ashamed of, or embarrassed about. But was it really something he would be desperate to get?

Lucy shook her head. She didn't think so. There had to be something more on the tape.

Now she was at the part where her VCR had gone on the blink.

The party was gone. It was a different setting now. A different day.

More sky. A few puffy clouds. Treetops — the leaves were just beginning to turn. Nothing to hide in this shot.

Suddenly, with a shaky swoop, the camera panned down from yellowing leaves. Everything blurred for a second, then came into focus.

Allen had been in the park. Lucy recognized the little stone bridge in the distance, and the water fountain along the path. The picture got wobbly; Allen was walking now.

Lucy saw kids playing, dogs romping, people strolling. Allen practiced zooming — she saw a lot of blurred faces or blobs of color that turned out to be sweatshirts.

Finally, he stopped walking and just turned in a semicircle. Then he stopped turning and held the camera steady.

Lucy squinted at the monitor. In the distance, she could see a small hill with two blobs of color on it. She waited, wondering if Allen was going to zoom in.

The camera zoomed, too much at first. More blurred faces.

Then Allen got it right. And Lucy saw what he had seen that day at the park.

Two people were on the hill. Leaning back against the grass, their arms wrapped tightly around each other, their lips locked together.

The couple didn't break apart, but they didn't have to. Lucy recognized them both.

Suzanne Gold, sitting on a hill in the park, passionately kissing someone.

But it wasn't Brad, the guy she'd been going with for so long.

It was Dave Travis, the guy Lucy had seen her with in the parking lot the day Jenny was attacked.

Chapter 14

Lucy stopped the recorder and stared at the image frozen on the monitor.

Was that the answer? Suzanne and Dave?

Now that she'd seen the two of them on tape, Lucy thought she understood why Suzanne had been in such a strange mood lately.

She could almost hear Suzanne saying, "I don't see how you can stand to watch it." She'd been talking about Allen's tape, and she'd said she couldn't watch it herself because it would make her think of him. She tried to make Lucy feel ghoulish for watching it.

Did she really expect Lucy to say, "Yeah, you're right, I'll throw it out?" Maybe.

But when Lucy didn't do that, Suzanne . . . what did Suzanne do?

Lucy remembered her date with Jon. Waiting for him to come back from driving his brother home. Suzanne on the phone to someone, saying, "You said you'd take care of it."

That was the night Lucy thought someone might have been in the house. Because the garage door was up. The tape hadn't been taken, though. If someone had gone in the house, they would have found it. Maybe. It wasn't labeled. So maybe not.

Anyway, it couldn't have been Suzanne. It had to be whoever she'd called.

Dave Travis. Suzanne would want to keep Brad from learning what was on that tape. Had Dave told Suzanne he'd "take care of it"?

Suzanne could have gone through Lucy's bag, though. That day when Lucy was waiting for Jenny, waiting right here, Suzanne had shown up to apologize for the way she'd acted in the office. And she'd stared at Lucy's duffel bag. Stared at the rip, or tried to see if Allen's tape was in it?

And the reason Suzanne had acted so defensively in the office, Lucy remembered, was because Lucy had said something about how people working there could get someone's locker combination.

It all fit.

Except maybe Dave. Would Dave really attack Lucy, just to get that tape for Suzanne? That's what he thought he'd done when he went after Jenny. *If* he'd done anything at all.

Leaning forward, Lucy put her elbows on the table in front of the monitor and stared at the screen. The picture was still frozen on the shot of Suzanne and Dave, wrapped together on the hill in the park.

Lucy shut off the monitor and put her head in her hands, thinking.

How would Suzanne even know about the tape? Would Allen have told her?

With a sigh, Lucy realized he would. Not to be mean, really. To tease. Allen loved to tease. Most people didn't mind, probably not even Suzanne.

Until he teased her about Dave. That wasn't something Suzanne would laugh about, not if she wanted to hide it from Brad.

Allen had been her friend, though. She must have asked him for the tape, or asked him to erase that part. And Allen had probably agreed. But then he'd died, and the tape had wound up in Lucy's hands. And Suzanne panicked.

Lucy sighed again, not knowing whether she was right or wrong.

It was time to keep going. Time to see if there was something else on the tape.

Lifting her head, Lucy reached for the control buttons. Then she froze, her hand in the air.

She'd heard something. This time she was sure of it.

Not the squeak of the door. Looking down again, Lucy could see that the door hadn't budged.

But she'd heard something — a click, almost like one of the machines being turned on or off.

Lucy decided to do the normal thing. She called out.

"Hi," she said. "Anybody there?" It could be anyone, she thought. It could be the guy who'd talked to her for half an hour before. It could be a custodian. She called out again.

It was the normal thing to do, but her voice sounded anything but normal.

No one answered anyway.

But Lucy knew she'd heard something.

Standing up again, she walked softly from behind the shelves, her head swiveling back and forth as she tried to take in the entire room at once.

Nobody.

She squeaked the door open and looked into the hall.

Nobody.

Then she noticed the big closet, where she'd found the tape. Someone could be in there. Hiding. Or maybe not. Maybe just getting something.

Still walking softly, holding her breath, Lucy went closer to the closet. She was ready to run if she saw anyone, even someone totally innocent. But she didn't have to run. The closet light was on, and no one was inside.

Lucy let out her breath and realized her knees were shaking. Maybe it was time to quit for now.

Just as she turned to go back to the table, she remembered something: the copy. Jenny's mother said Jenny had made a copy of the tape, and they were both all right.

The copy must be in the closet. It had probably been right next to the original.

Giving herself a shake, Lucy walked into the closet and looked. She remembered where she'd found the original, and right next to the spot was another unlabeled tape. They'd both been on the highest shelf, probably so no one would take them down and record over them by accident.

Lucy reached up.

She had to go up on tiptoe, and even then she had to stretch her arm way over her head.

That's how she was standing when she heard the sound.

Not a click this time. Sort of a grating sound.

Lucy gasped and started to turn around. But she was off balance, and she couldn't move as fast as she wanted.

Struggling not to fall, Lucy heard a whooshing sound.

And the closet's heavy metal door swung shut behind her.

"Hey!" Lucy had gained her balance now, and she grabbed the inside door handle. It wouldn't turn. "Hey!" she shouted again, slapping the door with her palm. "There's somebody in here!"

In spite of everything she'd just been thinking — about who might be after the tape — she honestly thought that someone had accidentally slammed the door on her.

But she didn't think that for long.

"Hey!" She hit the door again, this time using her fist.

No answer, no rush to open the door, no red-faced video student apologizing.

Silence.

Lucy strained her ears. Not silence after all. She heard movement; quick, light footsteps walking around the lab. Soft and quiet, though.

Whoever it was probably had sneakers on. Which didn't tell her anything.

Leaning against the door, Lucy held her breath and listened.

The footsteps stopped, at least she thought they did. She didn't hear anything for a few seconds.

Then, very faintly, a click.

Of course. The eject button. Lucy could almost see Allen's tape sliding out, into a waiting hand.

Whose hand?

Footsteps again, faster this time. He — she? — was leaving. Just walking away. No scratches on the arm this time, nobody hurt. This was a lot easier than mugging somebody on the street. Feeling a surge of anger at what had happened to Jenny, and at what was happening now, Lucy pounded on the door again. "Listen, you jerk. Hear that pounding? Somebody else'll hear it, too, you know. You'd better hurry, or you'll get caught. Go ahead!" she shouted. "Run, you creep!"

Catching her breath, Lucy leaned against the door and listened. No running footsteps; not that she really expected to hear them.

He was probably already gone. She'd probably been shouting to an empty room.

Then, without a sound, the closet light went out.

Almost immediately, Lucy heard a squeak and she knew what it was. The lab door had been shut. She couldn't hear the footsteps receding down the hall, but she followed them in her mind: down the hall, around the corner, down another hall or two, and out of the building.

If Lucy had been able to follow, she would have seen that she was right. Tape stuffed into a jacket pocket, her "stalker" walked quickly, but not quickly enough to attract attention. Away from the lab, down the hall past the gym, down another hall, and out into the late afternoon air.

It was November now, and getting cold. If Lucy had been there, she would have seen her stalker's breath in the air. It was starting to get dark, too, but not as dark as it was in the closet.

If Lucy had been able to follow, she would have seen her stalker smile and walk away in the cold November air.

But Lucy couldn't follow.

She was locked in the closet, alone. In the dark.

*　　*　　*

After a few seconds of listening with her ear against the door, Lucy tried the handle again. A waste of time. The door hadn't miraculously unlocked itself.

Frustrated, she slapped the door, then turned around and leaned against it.

Light. Light would help. Turning back, she ran both hands along the wall around the door, looking for a switch. The wall was rough, painted-over cinder blocks that scratched her fingers. There wasn't much wallspace anyway; the shelves covered all four walls of the closet except for about six inches on either side of the door.

And Lucy couldn't feel a light switch anywhere along those six inches. She slid her hand behind the shelves as far as she could. Nothing.

Maybe an overhead light, with a string. Standing on tiptoe again, she waved a hand in circles over her head. Moved forward a little and waved some more. No light string.

The only light switch was in the main room, and Lucy couldn't get to it.

Were all the lights out? Pressing her face against the edge of the door, Lucy tried to see if any light was coming through the crack. But the door fitted too well. She got down on her knees and looked for a sliver of light coming underneath. All she saw was darkness.

Light didn't really matter that much after all, she tried to tell herself. Getting out was what mattered.

But the lab door was closed, the closet door was locked, and all the lights were off. Unless a video student came to do some work, or the custodian came to clean, she was stuck.

For how long?

If she wasn't home by around dinnertime, and hadn't left a message, her parents would start to worry. Then they'd start calling around, trying to find out where she was. They'd try Jenny, who wasn't there. They'd try some other kids, but nobody they'd call had seen Lucy come in here.

Would they call the police next? Maybe. Or maybe somebody from the school first, like the vice-principal. Either way, the school would be searched, wouldn't it? Even if it wasn't, Lucy would be found when it opened again tomorrow.

Except there wasn't any school tomorrow.

Tomorrow there was a teachers' conference — a big district meeting at some hotel conference room, an all-day thing. Lucy had forgotten.

But her parents would still be calling to find her tonight, she reminded herself. Even if they were late getting home — Lucy stopped, remembering. Her father had gone out of town on business. He'd taken a plane, so Lucy had been able to drive his car to school that day. And her mother? Just this morning, her mother had told her she was going shopping after work with a friend, then to a movie. She wouldn't be home until nine or nine-thirty.

But then she'd start calling, Lucy told herself.

The whole thing might take a little longer, but Lucy would still be found.

Okay. All Lucy had to do was get through the night, and maybe part of tomorrow.

Leaning back, Lucy slid down the closet door until she was sitting, propped against it, her arms wrapped around her knees.

If only it wasn't so dark. She couldn't even make out the shelves in this darkness.

It was cold, too, and stuffy. Airless.

With a start, Lucy pushed herself back up until she was standing. Of course the closet seemed airless. Jenny told her it had been built as airtight as possible, to keep out moisture and dust. Lucy remembered laughing, saying they treated their tapes like rare jewels. It wasn't funny now.

The closet couldn't be completely airtight, though. Or could it?

Hands in front of her, she walked forward until she touched the shelves on the rear wall. Then she walked back, arms out to her sides, her fingertips just grazing the side shelves.

She guessed the closet was about six feet by ten feet. Sort of like a cell, she thought with a shudder. How long could a person last in a space like that without much air?

The more she thought about air, the more Lucy felt as if she couldn't breathe. In spite of the chill in the closet, she could feel the sweat beading on her forehead. She turned around and hammered her fist on the door. Even when she heard her breath coming in gasps and knew she was using up air, she kept hammering.

In the back of her mind, she knew it was useless, but she couldn't make herself stop. It was only — what? About five? Five-thirty? She'd heard basketball practice in the gym; it could still be going on. If she pounded hard enough, maybe someone would hear.

She could yell, too. She should have done

it sooner. Yelling a little wouldn't use up that much air, would it?

Still pounding, Lucy opened her mouth and yelled as loudly as she could. Once, twice, a third time, until she was gasping even harder.

Almost in tears now, Lucy leaned her head against the door and tried to get her breathing under control. She was breathing too fast, using up too much air. She had to stop.

Her breathing was the only sound she could hear in the dark, stifling space. In and out. Loud at first, then gradually softer and softer until she almost couldn't hear it anymore unless she tried.

Then, in the quiet darkness, Lucy heard another sound.

A squeak.

Someone had pushed open the outside door.

Chapter 15

Lucy's first instinct was to shout out, but something made her stop. Had he come back, whoever he was? Or she? Lucy reminded herself, thinking of Suzanne. Had she realized that Jenny, thorough Jenny, would make a copy of Allen's tape? Had the stalker come back to get it?

But whoever it was didn't want to be seen, and wouldn't come back knowing Lucy was still in the closet. Besides, Lucy wanted out. She'd risk it. She had to.

"Hello!" Lucy cried, pounding on the door again. "Hey, I'm stuck in here! Hello!"

Like magic, the light came on.

Then a voice, muffled, said something.

Lucy stopped pounding and leaned her ear against the door. Footsteps, fast ones, heading toward the closet.

Then the sound of a lock being turned.

The handle rattled and then the door swung open.

Jon was standing there.

With a gasp, Lucy rushed past him, out of the closet and into the big, bright, air-filled lab.

"I thought that sounded like your voice," Jon said as Lucy turned around to face him. "What happened? How did you get stuck in there? Are you okay?"

Lucy barely heard his questions. Her mind was racing with questions of its own. What was Jon doing here? He didn't have anything to do with the video group. Why had he just happened to walk into the lab right now? He had a job. Why wasn't he at work?

"Lucy?" Jon asked, staring at her curiously. "What's going on?"

Lucy pushed back her hair and wiped her forehead. Her hand came away smudgy. "I guess the closet's not dust-free after all," she said.

Jon still stared, looking confused and a little annoyed. "Hey, Lucy, come on," he said. "I come in here and hear you yelling and you're not even going to tell me what happened?"

Was he that good an actor? Lucy wondered. Or should she trust him?

No. She couldn't trust him. He might be the one.

"I . . ." Lucy cleared her throat and tried out a laugh. If was more of a croak, so she tried again. "Can you believe it?" she said. "Jenny asked me to come down here and put one of her tapes away and when I was in the closet, the door swung shut behind me."

She stopped for a second, remembering the door. It had been wide open when she'd gone into the closet. Whoever shut it must have been hiding behind it, waiting. Was she looking at that person right now?

Jon took hold of the closet door and pulled it wide. When he let go, it stayed where it was. He turned back to Lucy. "Are you sure that's what happened?" he asked.

"Well, sure . . . I mean, no! How could I be sure?" Lucy said, her voice rising. What did he want her to do, come right out and ask if he was the one who'd done it? "All I know is it shut on me. I guess the lock was already turned or something and I couldn't get out."

Jon looked at the door again, checking the lock. Then he looked back at Lucy, frowning. "How come you keep staring at me?"

Lucy felt her face get warm. She blinked and looked away. "I wasn't. I didn't mean to." She tried another little laugh. "I'm really glad to be out, thanks. What are you doing here, anyway?" she asked, hoping she didn't sound as if she suspected him of anything.

Jon kept frowning at her. "I wanted to talk to you," he said.

Without really meaning to, Lucy took a step back. Then she just kept going, around the shelves toward the table where she'd been watching the tape. "Oh?" she asked. "About what?"

Jon was right behind her, then he stopped and stared. Lucy followed his gaze. He was looking at her jacket, draped over the back of the chair, and at her bag on the floor beside it. He knew she hadn't been here just to put something away. But if he was the one who shut her in the closet, then he knew that anyway.

Lifting his eyes from the bag, he said, "I wanted to talk to you about something personal."

Suddenly, Lucy was afraid he was going to tell her everything he'd done — followed her, sneaked into her house, into her locker, attacked Jenny. She couldn't let him. If he told her, then what would he do to her?

Quickly, Lucy grabbed her jacket and bag. "I've got to get out of here, Jon," she said. "Being stuck in that closet really shook me up. I need fresh air."

She had to pass by him to get out, and she held her breath as she did, afraid he'd grab her arm.

Jon didn't move, though, and Lucy almost ran to the door.

"Lucy!" he called after her.

In the doorway, knowing she could get away now, Lucy felt safe enough to stop. Whirling around, she said, "If you wanted to talk to me, you could have called. From work — isn't that where you're supposed to be?"

"I did call," Jon said. "Nobody was home."

"Well, I don't have anything to do with the video lab!" Lucy said. "So how did you know where to find me?"

Jon took a step toward her. He opened his mouth to say something, but Lucy didn't wait to hear it. She spun out of the doorway and ran through the halls, out into the cold air.

She didn't feel safe until she pulled her father's car into the garage at home.

*   *   *

Friday. No school. Lucy spent the morning trying to sleep. Trying to forget what had happened to her the day before.

She still didn't know if Jon was the one, but why else would he show up in the lab so conveniently?

Good question, she thought. Why *would* he do that? Maybe he thought there might be a copy. Maybe he'd taken pity on her and decided to pretend he'd just happened by.

He said he'd called her. When she got home yesterday, breathless, halfway to panic, there'd been a hang-up on the answering machine. It could have been Jon. It could have been anybody.

Lucy wanted to trust him, but she was afraid to. She couldn't trust anyone who might go after her on a dark, rainy night.

Turning over in the bed, Lucy dislodged Moe, who was a heavy lump on her feet. He moved up to the pillow and purred directly into her ear. His breakfast call.

With a groan, Lucy finally got up, washed, and went into the kitchen. While the cat was eating, she sat at the table and drank some juice, thinking. She had to decide what to do.

There was a good chance that the copy of Allen's tape was still at school. Even if that's why Jon had come back, he probably couldn't have found it. There were hundreds of tapes in that closet, and not all of them were labeled. If it wasn't Jon, if it was one of the others, then they might not know about it or be able to find it, either.

She could get it and destroy it, Lucy thought. Then she could make sure everyone who mattered knew what she'd done. That would solve everything. She'd be safe, nobody else would get hurt, the whole thing would be over.

But if she did that, she'd never know why someone was after it. And she'd never know who.

An hour later, Lucy pulled her father's car to a stop in the student parking lot. There were only three other cars there. But something was always going on, even if there weren't any classes. The three other cars meant she'd be able to get inside the building.

As she passed the auditorium, Lucy heard laughter and peeked inside. Play rehearsal. No teacher, but some of the students were working on their own. She left the door and went on, her footsteps echoing in the empty halls.

The door to the video lab was closed, but not locked. The room was dark. Lucy flipped on the lights and pulled the door shut behind her. The squeak was gone, she noticed. Nervously, she walked around the room, looking behind shelves and making sure no one else was there, especially in the big closet. Empty.

Satisfied, Lucy went back to the hall door and locked it. No one could get in now, and she could do what she came to do.

The copy of Allen's tape was still on the upper shelf of the closet. At least, she thought it was the copy. She'd have to look to make sure.

Back at the table where she'd sat yesterday, Lucy turned on the equipment and slid the tape into the slot of the VCR.

The car wash appeared on the screen. This was it, the copy no one else knew about. Maybe.

Lucy reached out and stopped the tape. For a second, she thought again about destroying it. It would be very easy to do. But too much had happened because of this tape. She had to find out why.

Pressing play again, Lucy hunched forward and watched as the tape began to roll.

Just in case she'd missed something crucial, she watched from the beginning. The scenes were familiar now, but she kept looking for something different, something she hadn't seen before.

Nothing. There was nothing that looked strange or out of place. Except Jon's angry face.

And Suzanne in the park, with Dave Travis.

If only Jon hadn't shown up here yesterday, Lucy thought. Out of the blue, when he was supposed to be at work. If only he hadn't done that, she wouldn't think he was the one. She'd think it was Suzanne and Dave.

Maybe it was.

But there was more on the tape.

After Suzanne and Dave, Allen aimed the camera at a group of kids tossing a Frisbee. Little kids, not anybody Lucy knew.

Then there was a shot of Lucy, raking leaves. A new day, Lucy thought. Not long before Allen died. She hadn't even known he was shooting then. The camera moved in close to a shot of her cat, hunkered down, getting ready to pounce on the dry leaves fluttering across the grass.

A lot of snow and wavy lines appeared on

the monitor, and Lucy thought she'd reached the end of the tape. She was just about to stop the machine when the screen cleared and another scene appeared.

Dim. The light was dim and Lucy wasn't sure what she was seeing at first. After a few seconds, she realized she was looking at more trees. The park again?

Allen was walking and the camera jiggled a lot, but Lucy was able to make out twisted branches and thick underbrush. A wilder place than the park.

Then the trees gave way to a clear space, and Lucy recognized where Allen had been walking. It wasn't that far from where they lived, but it was like another world. The street they lived on was a dead end, giving way to an overgrown, undeveloped area thick with trees. They'd named it High Branch Forest when they were little, and they'd trampled a path in it, a path that eventually led to the top of a hill.

That was where Allen had stopped walking, at the top of the hill. He must have taken his camera there to get a panoramic shot. The hill looked down on a twisting dirt road that almost no one used anymore.

Someone was using it now, though. Or had been using it then, the day Allen had taken his camera there. Looking at the screen, Lucy could see a figure walking along the road, kicking up little clouds of dust.

The camera zoomed in. It wasn't like in the movies, a super close-up, but Lucy was able to tell that the walking figure was a man, wearing a reddish-colored cap, a brown windbreaker, and jeans. His head was down, so she couldn't see his face. He was walking slowly, kind of shuffling along. Almost weaving.

The camera stayed on the man for a few seconds. Then it swept past him, down the empty road, then back to the man. Lucy shifted impatiently, getting bored.

Maybe Allen had gotten bored, too, because the camera started to turn, back to the trees where he'd come from.

Then suddenly, it swept around to the road again, past the walking man.

The road wasn't empty anymore. A car was coming, and Allen kept the camera on it. He wasn't using the zoom anymore, and the camera was jiggling around, but not enough to ruin the shot.

The shot was perfectly clear. It had happened over a month ago, but Lucy felt as if it were happening now. Safe in the video lab, she watched the screen in horror, and saw what Allen had witnessed and recorded just a few days before his death.

Chapter 16

The car appeared on the screen in silence but Allen must have heard it coming. That must be why he'd turned the camera back to the road, Lucy thought.

It happened quickly.

The man was still walking, weaving into the center of the road. The car was moving fast, too fast to slow down.

Even though it took place in silence for Lucy, she could almost hear the screeching brakes, the thud as the fender hit the man, the scream as he flew through the air and landed hard on the edge of the road. She could almost hear the panicked breathing of the driver, and the crunch of gravel as the car finally skidded to a stop.

She thought it was over now. She expected Allen to toss the camera aside and run to help and she wouldn't see any more.

Instead, the camera stayed focused on the scene below.

Why? Lucy couldn't believe it. Why hadn't Allen gone down the hill to help?

In another few seconds, Lucy had her answer.

The man by the side of the road didn't move. But the car did. As Lucy watched, it backed up to the edge of the road, pulled out, and drove away.

Now the screen went blank. Lucy knew Allen had gone down to help the man, the victim of the hit-and-run driver.

But not an unknown driver. Because when the car backed up, Lucy was paying more attention to it than she had been before. And she recognized it.

And as the car pulled away, she caught a glimpse of the driver's face. She recognized it, too.

Allen must have recognized the driver immediately. Lucy could almost feel his horror as he stood there frozen, the camera running, steadier than it had ever been, filming a friend as he drove away from a hit and run.

A friend named Robert.

Lucy shut off the equipment. She closed her eyes, but the scene kept playing in her mind —

the man's shuffling walk, the blue car's speed, the grim set to Robert's jaw as he drove away. Robert had stared straight ahead, too intent on getting away to notice Allen, up on the hill.

The man had died, Lucy remembered now. Her mother had read it in the paper one morning and mentioned it. A hit-and-run death. The police had no leads; no one had come forward.

But Allen knew who'd done it, and now Lucy knew, too. Robert Owen, the smart one, the superachiever, the one who never failed.

Robert must have been terrified, Lucy thought. Hitting someone would ruin everything, even if it had been an accident. He probably had decided it was safer to run and hope that nobody would ever find out.

And nobody would have, if Allen hadn't been there.

Allen was there, though, and Lucy realized he must have told Robert. Of course he would. Allen wasn't perfect, but he wouldn't let a man be killed and not say anything.

But Allen was Robert's friend, too. So he told him what he'd seen and taped. He probably thought Robert would go to the police then.

Maybe Robert would have, if Allen had lived.

But Allen had died, and Robert was safe.

Except for the tape. Looking back on that night when she'd first gone through Allen's stuff, Lucy remembered thinking she'd seen a light in Allen's dark house.

Her imagination, she'd thought. Or ghosts.

But now she knew. It was Robert, looking for the tape that could ruin him. Not knowing that it was just across the yard, in Lucy's house.

Then he'd learned she had it, and he'd set out to get it. He'd finally done it yesterday, after slamming her in the closet. He must think he was really safe now.

But Robert still wasn't safe, because Lucy had a copy.

Lucy put her head in her hands, wishing she'd destroyed the tape instead of watching it. Now that she'd seen it, she couldn't pretend she hadn't. She had to do something about it, but what?

She couldn't just tell Robert. After what he'd done to get it, she was afraid to.

Her parents, she guessed. She'd go home, wait for her mother, and tell her everything. Her mother would tell her to call the police, and Lucy knew that's probably what she'd do, anyway. But not yet. First she wanted to go home.

With a sigh, Lucy pushed the button and the tape slid out. She held it in her hand for a moment, staring at it, wishing she'd never seen it.

She stood up, pulled her jacket from the back of the chair, and walked out from behind the shelves.

Robert was standing just inside the door.

He didn't say anything. He didn't move. He just stood there, looking at the tape in Lucy's hand.

Lucy's heart started drumming and her mouth went dry. How had he gotten in? She'd locked the door.

As if he'd read her mind, Robert held up his hand. In his fingers was a key. Finally, he spoke. "When you're a top student," he said, "they trust you with things like keys."

With his hand up, his sleeve slipped back, and Lucy saw three scratches on the back of his arm. They looked red and sore. Jenny had put them there.

Except for slipping the key into his jeans pocket, Robert still didn't move.

Lucy took a step back, anyway, and bumped

into the shelf behind her. She kept her eyes on Robert, not sure what he'd do.

"Come on, Lucy," he said. "I know you've seen the tape. I can tell by the look on your face. You might as well say what's on your mind before you give it to me."

Lucy wasn't ready to talk about that yet. "How did you know I was here?" she asked. "How did you know there was a copy?"

Robert sighed, as if she should be able to figure it out for herself. "I didn't know for sure that there was a copy," he said. "I know Jenny, though. She always makes backups. So after I left yesterday, I thought about it all, and I asked myself, 'What was Lucy doing in the closet?'"

Smart Robert, Lucy thought sarcastically. "What did you do, follow me here?"

He nodded. "Actually, I was on my way here, anyway. You turned in before I did, so I drove on by, waited a while, and came back." He sighed again. "I guess I waited a little too long. If I'd come sooner, maybe you wouldn't have seen what you did."

"Even if I hadn't seen it, I still wouldn't have given it to you," Lucy said. "The minute you asked for the tape, I would have known you were the one who was after it all along. Unless you weren't going to ask," she added. "Unless you were planning to shut me in the closet again."

Robert looked over at the closet. Its door was open wide, like yesterday. "I don't think something like that'll work a second time," he said, smiling slightly.

The smile made Lucy furious, and she bit her lip to keep from screaming at him. As calmly as she could, she asked, "What happened?"

"I was going to ask you the same thing," Robert said. "Who let you out, the custodian?"

"Jon found me, but that's not what I meant." Lucy took a deep breath. "I mean, what happened that day, with your car? Why didn't you stop after you hit that man?"

He shook his head impatiently. "You ought to know the answer," he said. "I can't afford to have something like that on my record. I've already got academic scholarships to four colleges. All I have to do is choose which one. Things are going great and they'll get even better. But not if something like that comes out."

"But it was an accident!" Lucy said. "I saw the tape, remember? He was practically in the middle of the road!"

"And I was going way too fast," Robert told her. "I couldn't stop or swerve because I was going too fast. Don't you think the police would have figured that out? I was the only car on the road, and I couldn't miss him? They would have laughed at me and written me up. Not for speeding, either."

"You couldn't be sure of that."

"No, and that's why I decided to run," Robert agreed. "Because I couldn't be sure."

Lucy couldn't think of anything to say.

"He was dead, Lucy," Robert said. "Even if I'd stopped, I couldn't have helped him."

"How do you know that?"

"Allen told me."

Lucy stared at him.

"Allen went down the hill after I drove away," Robert went on. "The man was dead. Allen told me so."

"Allen told you something else, too, didn't he? He told you he'd filmed it. I'll bet he told you to go to the police."

Robert's lips curved up again. "He told me more than that, Lucy."

"What do you mean?" Lucy asked. "What else would he say? He wouldn't tease you about it, not about something like that."

Robert was shaking his head, looking annoyed that she didn't understand what he meant. "He told me if I didn't, then he'd have to go himself."

Of course, Lucy realized. Allen wouldn't be able to just forget about it, not even for a friend. Poor Allen, she thought suddenly. What an awful choice to have to make.

"So you told him you'd do it, didn't you?" she asked bitterly. "But then Allen died. That was really convenient, wasn't it? You must have felt great."

"I didn't feel great," Robert said softly.

"Oh, right, I forgot," Lucy said. "The tape. Allen had filmed the whole thing and you had to get the tape." She was talking fast and angrily. "So you broke into his house, and when you couldn't find it, you must have really started to panic. What if his parents decided to watch it?

Then I came along, talking about this tape Allen's mom gave me. So you went after me — my house, my locker, my duffel bag. My friend!" Lucy said. "Jenny was wearing my raincoat. That's how I knew someone was after me. Not really me, though. After something I had — the tape. That was pretty stupid, Robert. If you hadn't attacked her, I probably never would have figured it out!"

"Maybe not. But you'd still have the tape," he reminded her.

Lucy took another deep breath. Yes, and she still had the tape, right in her hand. She tightened her grip on it.

Robert looked at it. "Why don't you just give it to me, Lucy?"

"Because I know what's on it," Lucy said.

"So what? It happened weeks ago. The guy's dead!" Robert's voice rose. "He was a drunk anyway. I read it. Why do you think he was weaving around like that? What difference does it make now?"

"It's just . . . I don't know!" Lucy cried. "I just know it makes a difference. I couldn't forget it."

Neither one of them had moved. Robert was still by the hall door. Lucy was still at the shelves, her legs pressed up against them. Both of them were quiet for a moment.

Finally, Robert broke the silence. "You're just like Allen," he said sadly.

"What do you mean?"

"Stubborn. You're both stubborn."

"Being stubborn doesn't have anything to do with it," Lucy said.

"Okay. Preachy, then. How does that sound?" Robert asked. "I begged Allen for the tape, I begged him to keep quiet. And what did he say? 'Oh, no, Robert, I can't do that! It would be wrong!' "

"Allen never talked like that," Lucy said. "But anyway, he was right."

"See?" Robert almost laughed. "Preachy, both of you."

Then Robert's smile disappeared. "It made me mad," he said. "He knew it would ruin my life and he still had to play the honest citizen and try to tell me what to do. It made me mad," he said again.

Lucy swallowed nervously.

"You're the same, Lucy," Robert said, looking at her. "I guess I knew you would be, but I hoped you wouldn't. I hoped you'd see it my way."

"I can't," Lucy whispered.

"That's exactly what Allen said." Robert's gaze drifted for a second, as if he were seeing Allen. Then his eyes snapped back to Lucy's face. "And look what happened to him, Lucy."

Chapter 17

For a moment, Robert's words didn't make any sense.

And then, like a fist in the stomach, their meaning hit her.

She could feel Robert's eyes on her, watching her, as she struggled to think of something to say. She opened her mouth, shut it, shook her head. She had to be wrong, she thought. He couldn't have meant that. He was just trying to scare her.

Lifting her head, Lucy finally looked across the room. Robert was still watching her, and when she saw the look in his eyes, she knew she hadn't been wrong.

"You killed him?" she whispered. "You killed Allen?"

"Not exactly. I wouldn't put it exactly like that," Robert said.

"How would you put it, then?" Lucy asked,

her voice stronger now. "Don't play word games, okay, Robert? Just tell me!"

"I guess I don't have any choice," Robert said. "I didn't mean for that to come out, but since it did, I might as well go ahead and tell you." Crossing his arms, he leaned back against the closed door as if he were settling in for a little storytelling session.

Lucy stayed where she was. She could feel the sharp edges of the shelves against her legs and back, but she didn't move, not even to shift her weight. Except for feeling those sharp edges cutting into her, she would have thought she was in the middle of a nightmare.

"Well." Robert cleared his throat. "Allen called me, the day after . . . after it happened. It was a Sunday."

Lucy remembered. Allen had died on a Sunday. On Monday, it had been the talk of the school.

"He said there was something we had to talk about," Robert went on. "Asked me to meet him. He wouldn't tell me over the phone. He sounded kind of tense, but I still didn't guess what it was all about. I was pretty tense myself, of course, and I said, can't it wait? He said no, it was too important."

Robert uncrossed his arms and put his hands

in his pockets. "So, I met him and we went for a walk."

Up on that high, crumbling embankment, Lucy thought with a shudder.

"He didn't come right out and tell me at first," Robert said. "First he asked me a few questions — what was happening, how was it going, like that. I guess he wanted to give me the chance to tell him. I told him everything was going great but, by then, I'd already guessed that he knew."

"So you told him?" Lucy asked.

Robert shook his head. "No. I kept hoping if I just stonewalled it, he might back off and keep quiet. But he didn't. He finally told me."

Lucy swallowed dryly. "Then what happened?"

"Well, we talked," Robert said. "I told him how it happened, and he said don't bother, he already knew — he'd seen it. He even had it on tape. He knew it was an accident, he said, even though I'd been driving too fast."

"See?" Lucy couldn't stop herself. "It was an accident. Anybody would think so, even the police."

Robert ignored her. "I told him about college, my career, my life — all that stuff. He said he understood that, too. He kept saying it would be okay." Robert's mouth twisted. "For a minute, I thought he was on my side."

"He *was* on your side," Lucy said.

"Oh, sure," Robert said sarcastically. "He tells me to go to the police. He says if I don't, then he will. You call that being on somebody's side?"

"He was your friend," Lucy said.

Robert's eyes drifted away again. "I know that. But he was wrong. It wasn't happening to him. If it had been, he couldn't have said what he did."

Allen wasn't wrong, Lucy thought. But she didn't argue this time. What was the point?

"I told him he was wrong," Robert said. "I used every argument I could think of. I even begged him not to say anything. He was really upset. So was I. We were shouting, but there wasn't anyone around. Nobody could hear us."

Lucy swallowed again. Now she was going to find out how Allen had died.

"We were shouting," Robert said again. "Waving our arms at each other and yelling. Then — I don't really remember how it started — but there was some pushing. We were heading for a real fight. He shoved me, I shoved back." He stopped talking suddenly.

"He lost his balance?" Lucy asked. "Lost

his balance and fell. Is that how it happened?"

Robert nodded and took a deep breath. "It was an accident!" he whispered hoarsely. "If Allen were here, he'd tell you the same thing. It was an accident!"

He probably would, Lucy thought sadly. She felt terrible. For Allen. Even for Robert, who'd been living with two horrible secrets.

But when Lucy looked up into Robert's eyes again, her sorrow disappeared. The secrets were exposed now. She knew them both. Lucy's scalp prickled, and she shivered with fear.

Robert took his hands out of his pockets. "I'm tired of all this," he said. "Tired of worrying about it and talking about it." He held out one of his hands. "Why don't you just give me the tape, Lucy?"

Lucy's fingers were slick with sweat, but she held on to the tape.

"Just give it to me, and everything'll be okay," Robert said, still holding out his hand.

Okay? Lucy thought. Like it was okay with Allen? She could give Robert the tape, but then what? He wouldn't trust her to keep quiet. He had two secrets to hide now. He'd killed to protect one of them. He'd do the same thing for two.

"Give it to me, Lucy," Robert said again.

"I . . ." Lucy shook her head. She glanced around the room. No way out. "I can't," she said.

"Well." Robert dropped his arm. "Okay, then."

For a split second, Lucy actually thought he might turn around and leave.

But, of course, he didn't. Instead, he pushed away from the door and started toward her.

Lucy tried to back up, but the shelves were behind her. She slid along them, feeling them shake, until she came to the corner. Then she backed away, toward the table where she'd watched the tape, afraid to take her eyes off Robert.

He was still coming. Not fast, but steadily. He was right in front of the shelves now.

Still holding onto the tape, Lucy rushed forward and pushed at the shelves, trying to topple them onto him. But they were stacked with heavy equipment, and all they did was wobble.

As Robert came around them, Lucy ran to the other end. She grabbed hold of the shelves again. Something fell, an empty box or something, but the shelves stayed upright.

Then the tape slipped out of Lucy's hand and fell to the floor.

Robert heard it, and started walking faster.

Gasping, Lucy kicked at the tape. It clattered across the floor and slid under another table.

Let him have it, Lucy thought, and raced for the door.

But Robert was right behind her. The tape could wait. First he had to stop Lucy.

Hearing him close behind, Lucy spun away from the door. She started to run to the other side of the room, but her toe caught on a thick cable and she went sprawling on her hands and knees.

Scrambling up, she felt Robert's hand reach for her. His fingers brushed her hair. She screamed and twisted away, and jumped toward the far wall.

He was only halfway across the room from her now, and still coming toward her.

Lucy moved sideways, her arms stretched out against the wall. She tried to scream again, but her breath was coming in harsh gasps and she couldn't get enough air in.

Robert seemed perfectly calm, breathing normally. Until she looked in his eyes. Then she saw the desperation.

Still moving sideways, Lucy scrabbled along

the wall with her fingers, hoping to find something, anything, to throw at him.

Finally, her fingers closed around something round and smooth. She chanced a look.
It was a tripod, with three metal legs and an
attachment at the top where a camera would
go.

Lucy grabbed it and tried to get a good grasp
on the legs. It was heavy and awkward, but if
she could hit him with it, she might stop him
long enough to get out.

Seeing what she had, Robert moved faster.

Lucy stepped away from the wall and swung
the tripod back, like a baseball bat. Then, with
all the strength she had, she swung it forward,
aiming for Robert's head.

The tripod was too heavy. Lucy couldn't
swing it fast enough. All Robert had to do was
duck, and that's what he did.

But when he ducked, he lost his balance.
And Lucy saw her chance.

Letting the tripod crash to the floor, Lucy
ran forward, put her hands flat on Robert's
back, and pushed.

Robert stumbled, tried to turn, and Lucy
pushed again, harder this time. Hard enough
to send him crashing through the wide-open

door of the airtight, fireproof closet where he'd trapped her yesterday.

With a cry, Lucy grabbed the door and slammed it shut behind him. She heard him fall against the shelves inside, and then she heard his fists on the door. But by then, she'd already locked it.

Still gasping for breath, Lucy backed away from the closet. Robert was pounding now, and shouting her name, but she didn't answer. She got her jacket, then went around and slid the tape out from under the table where she'd kicked it.

When she pulled open the door to the hall, she could still hear Robert pounding. For a second, she turned around and looked at the closet.

Just before she left, she turned out the lights.

Chapter 18

Jon arrived at Lucy's house at seven o'clock, looking wary. No wonder, Lucy thought, remembering the way she'd acted with him before. But he managed to make polite conversation with Lucy's mother for a few minutes.

Then he and Lucy got in his car and drove to the same hamburger place he'd taken her before. He waited for their sodas to arrive, took a sip of his, and then said, "Okay. Tell me."

So Lucy told him. All about the tape, and Robert. What he'd done to Allen, and why. What he'd done to get the tape once he knew Lucy had it. The only thing she left out was the part about Suzanne and Dave in the park. That would be their secret. And hers.

"After I left Robert in that closet — " Lucy

stopped. "How did you know I'd be there yesterday, anyway?" she asked.

"I didn't," Jon said. "I called your house and there was no answer. I wasn't looking for you at school, but I had to go there because I'd left some stuff in my gym locker. I heard you when I walked by the video room." He grinned. "You never gave me the chance to tell you."

A simple explanation, Lucy thought, wishing she'd stuck around to hear it. "Well, anyway, after I left Robert there, I called the police," she said. "And I've spent the last few hours with them. I was afraid they wouldn't believe me, but they did, even before I gave them the tape. I didn't see Robert again," she added. "I'm glad. I had to do it, but I hated it."

Jon nodded, his gray eyes thoughtful and sympathetic.

Lucy blinked back some tears. "After I got home and started to recover, I had to call you," she said. "To explain. To apologize, I guess, for thinking you might be the one."

"You don't have to apologize," he said. "I can see why you wondered about me. Especially after the way I reacted about your locker." He smiled, a little sadly. "It's because of my brother," he said. "He sort of got in with the wrong crowd for a while. I don't know why, he's a good kid, but I guess he was feeling mad and mean. Anyway, this group liked to shoplift and swipe stuff and break into lockers. When you told me about yours," he explained, "I thought they'd decided to hit the high school. I thought he might be in on it."

Lucy smiled. "You said he got in with this crowd for a while," she said. "You mean he's out of it now?"

"Yeah, I think so," Jon said. "My mother and I sat him down and told him to shape up. I think he will. He never did anything, he just hung around with them. And I don't think he liked them very much anyway."

"Does he like baseball cards?" Lucy asked. "I still have Allen's."

"I forgot to tell you," Jon laughed. "I told him about them. He said they'd be great."

"Good. I'll give them to you Monday." Lucy drank some soda. "Last thing," she said. "About that tape of Allen's . . ."

"You want to know why I looked so mad," Jon said.

"Yeah," Lucy said nervously. "You didn't just look mad, you looked mean and furious."

Jon was smiling.

"It's not so funny," Lucy said. "It scared me."

"It was supposed to," he said. "Well, not scare *you*. It was supposed to scare my brother. I told Allen about him, how he was messing up. Allen said I ought to come down really hard on him, try to scare him into shaping up. I told him I couldn't do it. He said I should practice."

"Practice?" Lucy asked. "You mean, rehearse?"

"Right. So I did," Jon said. "Allen and I cracked up laughing after I'd finished, but you didn't see that part."

"I should have asked," Lucy said. "So, did it work? With your brother, I mean?"

"I never tried it," Jon admitted. "My mother and I just talked to him, like I said. No yelling or anything." He paused. "But Allen was just trying to help out. I wish I could have told him what happened."

Lucy felt tears starting again and concentrated on finishing her drink. When she'd sucked the last drop through the straw, she looked up and found Jon watching her. He was grinning again.

"What?" she asked.

"Does this count as a date?" he asked.

"I don't know," Lucy said, surprised. "Why?"

"Well, we're going out tomorrow night, too," he reminded her. He reached over and pushed her hair off her forehead. "I could get used to this."

Lucy took his hand and held it. "Me too," she said.

P•INT CRiME

If you like Point Horror, you'll love Point Crime!

A murder has been committed . . . Whodunnit?
Was it the teacher, the schoolgirl, or the best friend? An
exciting new series of crime novels, with tortuous plots and
lots of suspects, designed to keep the reader guessing till
the very last page.

Point

Pointing the way forward

More compelling reading from top authors.

The Highest Form of Killing
Malcolm Rose
Death is in the very air . . .

Seventeenth Summer
K.M. Peyton
Patrick Pennington – mean, moody and out of control . . .

Secret Lives
William Taylor
Two people drawn together by their mysterious pasts . . .

Flight 116 is Down
Caroline B. Cooney
Countdown to disaster . . .

Forbidden
Caroline B. Cooney
Theirs was a love that could never be . . .

Hostilities
Caroline Macdonald
In which the everyday throws shadows of another, more mysterious world . . .

THE UNDERWORLD TRILOGY
Peter Beere

When life became impossible for the homeless of London many left the streets to live beneath the earth. They made their homes in the corridors and caves of the Underground. They gave their home a name. They called it UNDERWORLD.

UNDERWORLD
It was hard for Sarah to remember how long she'd been down there, but it sometimes seemed like forever. It was hard to remember a life on the outside. It was hard to remember the real world. Now it seemed that there was nothing but creeping on through the darkness, there was nothing but whispering and secrecy.

And in the darkness lay a man who was waiting to kill her . . .

UNDERWORLD II
"Tracey," she called quietly. No one answered. There was only the dark threatening void which forms Underworld. It's a place people can get lost in, people can disappear in. It's not a place for young girls whose big sisters have deserted them. Mandy didn't know what to do. She didn't know what had swept her sister and her friends from Underworld. All she knew was that Tracey had gone off and left her on her own.

UNDERWORLD III
Whose idea was it? Emma didn't know and now it didn't matter anyway. It was probably Adam who had said, "Let's go down and look round the Underground." It was something to tell their friends about, something new to try. To boast that they had been inside the secret Underworld, a place no one talked about, but everyone knew was there.

It had all seemed like a great adventure, until they found the gun . . .

Also by Peter Beere

CROSSFIRE
When Maggie runs away from Ireland, she finds herself roaming the streets of London destitute and alone. But Maggie has more to fear then the life of a runaway. Her step-father is an important member of the IRA – and if he doesn't find her before his enemies do, Maggie might just find herself caught up in the crossfire . . .

POINT FANTASY

Read Point Fantasy and escape into the realms of the imagination; the kingdoms of mortal and immortal elements. Lose yourself in the world of the dragon and the dark lord, the princess and the mage; a world where magic rules and the forces of evil are ever poised to attack . . .

Available now:

Doom Sword
Peter Beere
Adam discovers the Doom Sword and has to face a perilous quest . . .

Brog The Stoop
Joe Boyle
Can Brog restore the Source of Light to Drabwurld?

The "Renegades" series:
Book 1: Healer's Quest
Book 2: Fire Wars
Jessica Palmer
Journey with Zelia and Ares as they combine their magical powers to battle against evil and restore order to their land . . .

Daine the Hunter:
Book 1: Wild Magic
Book 2: Wolf Speaker
Tamora Pierce
Follow the adventures of Daine the hunter, who is possessed of a strange and incredible "wild magic" . . .

Foiling the Dragon
Susan Price
What will become of Paul Welsh, pub poet,
when he meets a dragon – with a passion for
poetry, and an appetite for poets . . .

Dragonsbane
Patricia C. Wrede
Princess Cimorene discovers that living with a
dragon is not always easy, and there is a
serious threat at hand . . .

The Webbed Hand
Jenny Jones
Princess Maria is Soprafini's only hope
against the evil Prince Ferrian and his
monstrous Fireflies . . .

Look out for:
Daine the Hunter:
Book 3: The Emperor Mage
Tamora Price

Star Warriors
Peter Beere

The "Renegades" Series
Book 3: The Return of the Wizard
Jessica Palmer

Elf-King
Susan Price

POINT SF

Encounter worlds where men and women make hazardous voyages through space; where time travel is a reality and the fifth dimension a possibility; where the ultimate horror has already happened and mankind breaks through the barrier of technology . . .

The Obernewtyn Chronicles:
Book 1: Obernewtyn
Book 2: The Farseekers
Isobelle Carmody
A new breed of humans are born into a hostile world struggling back from the brink of apocalypse . . .

Random Factor
Jessica Palmer
Battle rages in space. War has been erased from earth and is now controlled by an all-powerful computer – until a random factor enters the system . . .

First Contact
Nigel Robinson
In 1992 mankind launched the search for extra-terrestrial intelligence. Two hundred years later, someone responded . . .

Virus
Molly Brown
A mysterious virus is attacking the staff of an engineering plant . . . Who, or *what* is responsible?

Look out for:

Strange Orbit
Margaret Simpson

Scatterlings
Isobelle Carmody

Body Snatchers
Stan Nicholls

Read Point SF and enter a new dimension . . .